Praise for the Base Branch Series

"Megan Mitcham's books are well-paced, well-plotted suspense novels edged with stunning sensual intensity. Her lovers are cold and deadly--except when they are skin-to-skin. I can't wait for the next book in the series!"

- DELILAH DEVLIN
New York Times and USA Today bestselling author

"Nail-biter all the way to the end."

- Michelle, MsRomanticReads
Adult Romance & Erotic Book Reviews

"This is a fresh and exciting story with lots of great characters."

- 5 Star Amazon Review, Enemy Mine

"Megan now joins my elite team of must read authors. I fell in love with her work in *Enemy Mine*, and it just gets better the more I read."

- TNT Reviews

BOOKS BY MEGAN MITCHAM

BASE BRANCH NOVELS
ENEMY MINE
JUSTICE MINE
STRANGER MINE
WARRIOR MINE
DANGER MINE
PRISONER MINE
VERSIONS
VIRTUES
VARIATIONS
SURVIVOR MINE - 2017

BUREAU NOVELS
FOR ALL TO SEE
PAINTED WALLS
FORD'S BOOK - 2017

ANTHOLOGIES
ANTICIPATION
CONQUESTS
ROGUES
SEX OBJECTS
COWBOY HEAT
HIGH OCTANE HEROES
WILD AT HEART VOLUME II
benefiting Turpentine Creek Wildlife Refuge

Virtues

Base Branch Novella #8

Megan Mitcham

Published by MM Publishing LLC

Edited by Lacey Thacker

Proofread by Tina Rucci & Lynn Mullan

Cover Design by Deranged Doctor Designs

Virtues
All Rights Are Reserved. Copyright 2016 by Megan Mitcham

Virtues

Second electronic publication: September 2016
Second print publication: September 2016

Digital ISBN: 978-1-941899-21-2

Print ISBN: 978-1-941899-20-9

For Diana, the lady with all the virtues,

Thank you for being my forever cheerleader. From teaching me to ride a bicycle—looking the other way when I hit the asphalt, and then popped up with an expletive—to devouring everything I've ever written, pushing me for more, and everything between. You're in my corner tried and true. Then there are the acts of love and kindness you perform for everyone else; visiting with the elderly, organizing craft nights, working at the church, adoring your children and husband while simultaneously keeping them in line, and last but not least, reminding everyone to laugh with your infectious smile and quips.

I appreciate you more than words can express!

Your niece,

Megan

Chapter One

Cara had only come back to protect her daughter. Anything more exposed her and put Rin in greater danger.

Why in the hell hadn't she stuck to the plan?

The buoyancy unparalleled to any she'd experienced in the last seventeen years—since she'd last held her daughter in her arms, smelled her sweet skin, and awed at her heartbreaking smile—it might as well have been another soul-crushing dream. A casual cough shook the room. It crumbled her hopes and eviscerated even the ghosts of her dreams.

How fitting to see the future, to touch it and cling to its warmth, only to have it ripped away. Cara had forfeited her life for her daughter long ago. Today, she would forfeit her future for Rin. For Rin and Luck.

Before she heard the heavy cough rumble to a stop, Cara drew the CZ from its holster, turned, and extended the barrel toward the man blocking the only exit in the one-room warehouse apartment. She was ready to take his bullet and deliver her own because he'd gotten the jump on her. Yet the slice of high-velocity metal slamming into her flesh didn't steal her breath. The casual smile, relaxed stance, and the sheer amount of high-tech weaponry hanging from his Kevlar vest sucked the air from her lungs.

Two feet behind Cara, Luck yanked Rin to his side, shielding her with his body. His draw was slow. His concentration divided between Rin and the situation. A situation they needed to vacate immediately.

Sweat rolled between Cara's shoulder blades and down the curve of her rigid spine. She righted her aim. Three yellow dots mounted atop her pistol lined up perfectly between the stranger's woodsy green eyes. Impressive, considering her usually easy grip had morphed into an unrelenting vise, and the tension at the base of her skull translated into a vicious migraine. Luck wasn't the only one divided here. When Cara needed her battle-honed body the most, it betrayed her.

"I sure didn't mean to break up a moment." The stranger offered work-roughened palms and jostled his hips, shifting his weight to one side. His dominant side. Cara watched his right hand and the steady pulse in his thick neck. The twang in his accent screamed of a tug on the brim of a sweat-stained Stetson and sweet tea.

This one was a snake charmer, all right. Too bad she was a mongoose.

"Move on and you may live to regret it." Luck always led with bravado, and he usually had the goods to back it up. Today, Rin was in the mix. This was no time for show. It was time for decisive action.

"I'm not here to cause trouble." The soldier cowboy's honeyed drawl matched his words, but she didn't trust anyone, not even herself.

"From my point of view, you're nothing but trouble." Cara cataloged the hint of a knife handle at his ankle, the blatant K-bar strapped to his left column thigh, and the Glock on his right hip.

"Cara Lee." The stranger said her name with a familiarity that hinted of intimacy. "More than most, you should know...looks can be deceiving."

He knew too much. Without permission, her throat quivered. She swallowed the words she'd counted on to get them out of there. If he knew her name, her ruse as a CIA operative wouldn't work.

"I'd like y'all to come with me." The bastard had the gall to offer his hand. She'd snap it off and toss it down the stairs as soon as she'd take it.

"No." Cara stepped diagonally, placing herself two feet closer to the enemy and between him and her children.

If Rin hadn't taken that job with the Department of Defense, Cara's old enemy wouldn't have dug up her false grave, figured out her trickery, and used Rin to find her. If Ansya Popov hadn't held a grudge like the Grim Reaper, Popov would still be alive, Cara would still be dead, and Rin would still be safe.

This wasn't the time for blame games. Though, currently, she blamed Luck for not following the plan. Damn her quasi-adopted son for falling in love with her baby girl and ruining everything. Double damn her for not realizing his adoration before she'd been able to pull him out of the field and off Rin's protection detail.

A small red dot slid up the end of Cara's nose and centered her brows, mirroring the bead she held on the wide-jawed stranger. He could probably take a bullet in that thing, waggle it, and go about the business of dismantlement. But he didn't hold the line on her. The laser came from beyond the doorway and through the wall of square glass panes. The sniper nested on a rooftop far enough away the shot impressed her, as long as it didn't splatter her brains on the walls with the pull of a trigger. Other dots accompanied the first. One landed on her boob before lifting to her heart. Go figure. Another lifted over her shoulder.

Rin, her baby girl who'd grown into a stunning and strong woman, whimpered. Cara's heart shattered. She'd caused the person she loved the most in this world so much pain.

Cara lowered her weapon slowly and placed it in her holster. "I'll go with you."

"No, please," Rin sobbed.

"I have a thing or two to say to Director Haskens." Cara blocked her daughter's plea and focused on the soldier cowboy.

"I don't work for the CIA." His lips pursed. Those big things could use their own rolling luggage, but they didn't look out of place on him. Probably because he was so big. Hell, she hadn't noticed them before. A thousand different thoughts and emotions were at play here, this non-CIA operative's kisser being the absolute least of those.

"Then who?" she demanded.

"Can't tell you. Not that you'd recognize it if I did." His sweet confidence puffed to cocky.

"Please." Cara snorted. The tension eased in her shoulders. She'd lived through an abusive marriage to the cheating man her government had trained her to seduce and betray. She could handle this kid. "I was dismantling a government while you were suckling your momma's breasts."

His thick brows knitted. A gaze far brighter than his drawl or years allowed shifted across her body, stinging every spot it rested.

"You've been on the run since I hit puberty." His arms spread as if offering her a good look at the specimen he'd become. "That's a damn long time to run. I can help you stop running."

"By killing me?" Cara pushed her words through gritted teeth because he'd hit too close to the truth. His words left bruises.

That wide jaw shook one determined time. "By stopping the people who are looking for you."

"I've already taken care of that." Popov would never again hurt her family.

"The CIA?" He tilted his head in assessment and then finally shook it. "I have no doubt you could disappear and no one would find you again, but you'd never get the chance to have a life with your daughter. She's the only reason you haven't tried to fight your way out of here already."

Her daughter. This man knew where to strike. It took almost no force. Just a whisper of precision and he had her on her knees. The only thing she wanted more than to spend hours, days, years with her daughter, the most beautiful creature on the entire earth, was to ensure Rin's safety.

"We can clear your record and make it safe for you to stay Stateside with Rin." The stranger's gaze didn't leave Cara's as he dangled the dream over a chasm she'd have to cross to get to it. Because nothing was free. Nothing was easy.

Her heart scaled her throat, finding footholds in the sensitive flesh and making it impossible to swallow. Her mind fought to block the tempting images. As war hardened her heart, the vision of Rin's blond hair pinned back with a veil, a simple bouquet clutched in graceful fingers, and her brilliant smile violated her resolve as though she were a hapless mark. She blinked the scene away.

The stranger's eyes hadn't moved, but his attention shifted. That intense weight lifted from her chest only to redouble. His interest had shifted over her shoulder to Luck and Rin.

"I'll go with you." Cara lengthened her spine and drew the brunt of his full scrutiny. "They stay."

"They come," he rebounded with little inflection. Her lips parted to rebut the point, but his head shook in one slow swing. "They ensure you won't run."

Every nerve in her system knitted, forming a suffocating blanket of mother fuck. This smooth-talking cowboy had her number. She might as well find out who'd given it to him before she vanished. "They go, but if you or your men hurt them in any way, my last act on this earth will be ripping your balls out of your sack and shoving them up your nostrils."

A high whistle came from the doorway. It belonged to a stout black man dressed in similar tactical gear. The bore of his pistol slowly swept the room. Big lips, almost as big as the cowboy's, puckered as the noise coalesced with the, "No shit!" of a third man in tactical gear who cluttered the doorway.

"She's all yours, Bulldogger." The black man's lips spread into a bright, amused smile.

The third guy, his blond hair pulled back into a low ponytail, chuckled. "Ditto." He held a shiny silver pistol pointed at Luck's chest.

Cara's gaze sliced back and forth between each of the guns and then back to Bulldogger... Whatever the hell kind of nickname that was.

"Noted, ma'am." He nodded.

"I might just do it because you called me ma'am." She glared.

"Sorry, ma'am. That's how we do things where I come from. Nice and gentleman like." His hips shifted, and his gaze lifted. "Damien Luck?"

Luck answered with a grunt.

"Man, I'm not going to hurt you or your lady love." For the first time, his gaze blatantly studied the other people with Cara. Before long, it jumped back to her and narrowed.

"All the rifles aimed at my chest really give that warm and fuzzy vibe," Luck smarted.

The cowboy held two fingers by his side for two seconds. In near synchronization, the dots vanished, and the two soldiers to his left holstered their weapons. Neither Cara nor Luck was green enough to think their respective chests didn't still overwhelm the sniper's scopes, but it was a gesture.

Those dark green eyes shifted behind her again. "I need you to drop your weapon."

"Do it," Cara ordered. What choice did they have?

The clank of metal on concrete filled the room.

"Kick it away, and then do the same to the rest of them." Bulldogger's heavy jaw jutted.

Scuffs and thunks littered the stale air, along with a curse or five as Luck removed his weapons.

Bulldogger nodded, glanced at his teammates, and canted his head toward Luck and Rin. The two walked past, giving her a wide berth.

"Cara?" His thick brows hiked as though saying, 'your turn.'

A plan formed on the outer rim of her brain and congealed at the center. It was risky, but what was life without a little risk? She didn't damn well know. Maybe one day. Then again, probably not.

Cara unholstered her CZ. With the barrel in her grip, she held it level and bent at the waist. The V of her soft cotton shirt gapped toward the floor, revealing the round tops of her breasts and a hint of her black lace bra. Her knees gave way to a crouch. She laid the pistol on the floor at arm's length, stood, and stepped away.

"Much obliged." His eyes sparked.

For a quarter of a minute, they stood and stared at one another. Triumph welled inside Cara's beating chest.

"Now for the rest of them." He grinned and indicated her lower half. "Ankle?"

"It was worth a try," she sneered.

"No complaints here." His grin morphed into a smirk.

She bent, yanked off her ankle cannon, holster and all, and hurled it at his feet. It hit the end of his boot and bounced off, spinning two complete rotations before coming to rest between them.

"Calf?" He pointed at her opposite leg.

A shuffle and tear at her pant leg revealed her eight-inch fixed blade. Again, she jerked off the weapon and tossed it at him.

"Midriff?" His gaze dropped to her middle.

"I thought you were a gentleman?" She glared.

"I'm not frisking you, but I have a feeling I'll have to before this is all said and done."

Pride pulled her to her full height, which, sadly, was about a head off his. Her arms spread wide. Meekly, she smiled.

Bulldogger smiled back, but there was nothing meek about it. The gesture shot adrenaline straight to her heart. Cara breathed steadily through her nose. He stepped forward and kicked the weapons farther from her reach. She didn't need them. Another step brought him within swinging distance. Her shoulders relaxed.

His tread-worn boot landed inches from hers. Cara struck. Her right arm rocketed toward his stern nose. She intended to stagger him, relieve him of his sidearm, and hold his big ass hostage.

Circulation in her wrist ceased. The room tilted, and she met the concrete in a blink. All the air in her lungs sailed out of her body with a hurricane force gust. The easy talking cowboy wrenched her hands behind her back and splayed himself across her body. His thick legs pinned her to the cold hard surface. Stars danced in her periphery, but at the center, Rin's mouth opened in a furious roar. Next to her, the lasers danced across Luck's chest once again.

Cara relaxed, forfeiting the first fight of her life with embarrassingly little effort.

"Don't feel bad," the cowboy whispered into her ear. "As soon as I got off my momma's teat, I started wrestling steer."

Now she knew why they called him Bulldogger. Fucking great.

Pressed against the chilly concrete, her cheek stung, almost as much as her pride. It wasn't the man's strength that skewered. His grip bit as much as any she'd endured. His forearms touted muscles as thick as her thighs. The irritating fact that he'd seen her attack coming miles before she'd moved jostled her front and center.

Had this easy talker really knocked the last of the fight out of her? Lord knew, she'd been fighting for too long. Cara didn't want to fight or run, but she would until Rin was safe.

She choked in several breaths. "Fine. I have blades on my waist and left thigh." Her right eye found Rin. "Stop fighting. I'm fine." Luck wrenched her daughter's clawing hand from his shirtfront, reeled her back to his side, and mumbled something into her hair.

Sandpaper roughened Cara's cheek. The cowboy's warm breath coasted over her jaw. "If you promise not to sling a blade in my neck or any other body part, I'll let you remove them yourself."

"Fine," she hissed again.

He stood and pulled her to her feet in one smooth move. The assist flipped the finger to her already damaged pride. She snapped an elbow against his ribs and quickly lifted her hands palm up to his buddies on the roof and in the room. To his credit, he only wheezed once and stayed upright, if not slightly hunched. No way he could help the red that flushed through his cheeks nor the bulge in the veins of his neck.

"You're damn determined to get frisked." He coughed.

"And you're determined to lose a part of your manhood." She glared.

Bulldogger stepped into the line of the lasers dotting her stomach. His angry green gaze left her and found his cohorts. He raised his index finger and whirled it. She looked back long enough to see the soldiers frown and then give her their backs. "You too," he barked. Luck and Rin balked. "Now."

When they turned, Cara faced the cowboy. "What about you?"

"So you can sever my spine? I don't think so."

He'd demanded more privacy for her than she had reason to expect, and they'd wasted enough time. Cara unbuttoned the snap of her slim fitting tact pants, freed the zipper, and pushed them over her hips. Gravity made quick work, plunging them to her ankles and giving her access to all her weapons. Too bad they didn't work anymore. The black lace of her bra hadn't enticed him. She doubted the matching boy shorts could. At forty-five, she'd officially lost her touch.

Ever the gentleman, Bulldogger didn't leer, but then again, his gaze didn't leave her body either. Probably scared of losing a ball. And rightly so.

She unbuckled the double straps from her taut thigh and tossed the sheath and two small knives to the floor. Cara hitched her shirt, unwound that strap from her middle, and tossed it and the single blade down with the others.

"Satisfied?"

"Turn."

Cara glared a hole through his forehead. He whirled that index finger again, while his neutral visage maintained a clinical interest. Still, it felt too intimate to be standing before only him in an open room full of people and guns. She slapped her long blond ponytail over her shoulder and swiveled on her heels, determined not to make anything of her unusual vulnerability. When her gaze lost his, and the mostly bare ass cheeks leveled on him, the humid air inside the old warehouse condensed on her back once more, threatening to give her away. Her feet shifted to complete the 360 with her pants around her ankles. The sooner, the better.

"Stop," he ordered.

Damn.

"I charge by the minute," she growled.

"Huh." The rumble of his harrumph rattled its way across the shell of her ear from mere inches away. Her ruffled ponytail shot over her shoulder and smacked her collarbone. Heat centered her spine as the back of his hand clamped the dagger strapped to the clasp of her bra, running up the center of her spine.

"I charge by the inch." The rumble of his growl reverberated against her cheek. He dragged the hot metal from its sheath, pulling the damp material away from her skin. Gooseflesh spread across her shoulder blades. The sharp point skimmed along her spine.

A shiver zipped every which way, except the way it should've...which was no-damn-where.

"Get dressed. Get all his weapons. Reassure your daughter." The harsh tread of his boots retreated two steps. Funny how they hadn't made a sound only moments ago.

Over the years, through the countries and conflicts, Cara met with harassment of all levels, but this man's subtle bedevilment provoked more than most. During the others, her daughter had been part of the equation, albeit a distant one. Now, Rin was in the thick of it.

Her hands itched to retaliate in some way or, at the very least, clench into stubborn fists. The need to shake them in the air and scream shrank her skin two sizes. Cara refused to let this errand boy see a glimpse of his aftermath. If only her SOP detachment would kick in. With a prim crouch, she pinched the top of her pants between her thumbs and forefingers and pulled with an exaggerated nonchalance that probably wouldn't fool a child. It certainly didn't fool her subconscious. The button slipped three times in her quaking digits. She lifted her chin, filled her lungs, and tried again. Sheer will forced the metal through the slot. Giving up on apathy, she jerked the cotton over her torso and stepped toward Luck.

"Ditch it all." He turned at her words. Hard lines accentuated his boyishly handsome features, revealing his history, the experiences no child should have to endure. Many of those same hardships her daughter had also endured. Cara's stomach cramped. When he didn't immediately move, she added, "Even the watch."

"Goddamnit."

Rin didn't flinch at Luck's severe tone. Her eyes followed each of the weapons he tossed to the ground in barely contained rage, but a strength Cara admired more than her own held Rin's reaction behind the unflappable mask of her beautiful, tear-stained face.

When Luck removed the last of his arsenal, vest and all, Cara held her hand out to her daughter. Blue eyes surveyed the men in the room. Rin's fingers formed a protective canon around her hand. Tears stung, but she wouldn't allow them to materialize. They wouldn't help anything.

"I'll make this right," Cara whispered.

"I can't live without either of you. Not anymore." Her voice caught. Tears gathered in her little girl's eyes and bruised her heart anew.

Cara dropped Rin's hand and turned toward the cowboy. "We're ready."

"Almost." Three black bags hung from his massive hands.

Chapter Two

"Christ, Tyler! You trying to drive like me? Not ideal when you've driven more cows than cars. We can switch. You know I love a high-speed"—he huffed—"anything. I like a high-speed anything when I'm buckled." In the rearview mirror—over the top of their three passengers' black bags—his teammate, Oliver Knight, braced an arm on the ceiling of the blacked out SUV.

"You're not buckled? You know that's against the law." Tyler took a hard right in the parking garage and barreled toward a concrete wall. The computer that scanned the car when they'd entered a story above cleared their cargo. It also laid down the newly added fortification. He zoomed over the large hump. Just last week, Oliver had gotten airborne on the thing. Now, his ponytail lurched while he resisted gravity's pull.

A deep chuckle erupted from the front passenger seat.

"Laugh it up, asshole." Oliver grinned. "Next time, you're riding back here, and I'm driving."

"Not a chance in hell. Your momma told me how many cars you've crashed. And I've seen you demolish a couple." Hunter Masters held firmly to the *oh-shit* handle. He carried on with Oliver, but his gaze swiveled between Cara Lee behind the driver's seat, Damien Luck in the middle, and Rin Lee behind him.

"That's only the ones she knows about." Oliver turned to watch the second SUV, carrying their sniper team, take the hump at the same speed. "Gate's up." His friend referred to the wall that slid into place after the second car cleared it as the gate. It had been a gate before...

In front of the elevators, Tyler cut the engine, got out, and tossed the keys to Hebert, who exited the second car. "Free Oliver for me, would ya?"

"We can't leave him?" Hebert asked.

"It's your hospital bill." Tyler nodded at Hunter. In unison, they opened the SUV's back doors.

"Damn right," Oliver called from the back. A second later, the hatch opened. "That's what I thought, Hebs."

"Up your ass, Ollie," Hebert groused.

"That's enough, fellas," Tyler rumbled.

"A gentleman once more?" Cara said the first thing since he'd presented her with the black bags and made her place one over her daughter's and apprentice's heads. "Funny how that comes and goes, along with the sound of your boots."

"Glad to see you're still breathing. Since we made it here without incident—incident meaning me bleeding out on the side of the road or suffocating to death—I wasn't sure."

Hunter retrieved Rin from the SUV and ushered her to the elevator. Oliver talked with Damien in a hushed tone. The capable man slid out of the car and shuffled forward. Shackles around his ankles rattled with each step. When they'd pulled out the restraints at the SUVs, which they'd parked in the alley outside the warehouse, Cara had nearly bounded the border of sane. They'd explained it was for all their safety. She hadn't given a shit. The only way they'd gotten them in the things without blood and sweat was bargaining. Rin hadn't had to wear them.

"Yet you didn't stop to check on my well-being. I'm hurt."

"You look it," he said with a chuckle.

Cara looked hot as tar at 3:00 p.m. on an August day. As dangerous too.

The cuffs he, himself, had fastened at the ankles of her long, lean legs and her svelte wrists sat in a pile on her lap under her daintily folded hands.

"What? They were chaffing." When she shrugged, the black bag bobbed.

She'd had to wait until they stopped and Hunter's and Oliver's attention was averted, but even then, she hadn't been out of sight for a full minute. Cara Lee wouldn't run. They had her daughter. This was a statement, and he could appreciate it.

"By all means, allow me." He scooped the heap of metal into his palm. The heat of her thighs seeped through his skin before he lifted the cuffs and tossed them onto the seat next to her.

"Why, thank you." Her sweet reply got his back up. She was up to something. He'd calculated all the angles and knew from here she could attack in multiple ways. It was what he did. Assessed risk. Mapped schemes. Minimized the good guys' exposure. It was why he wasn't a cattle rancher back home.

Cara turned toward him. The edge of her thigh brushed the front of his pants. She recoiled quickly, as though she hadn't meant to dry stroke him.

Not likely.

Her every action had a motive behind it. It was how she was wired and how she'd lived for so long on the run from the unrelenting remnants of the Soviet Union and the very active CIA.

Even so. He knew exactly how those toned legs looked without baggy tactical pants. The hot jolt of desire he'd battled while inspecting her for concealed weapons roared to life in the form of an unmistakable boner. Thank fuck she wore the bag. Too bad for his boner it was all part of her hook.

"Give me your pick," he demanded.

"I'd rather give you something else," she purred.

"Yeah, my balls as a nose plug. Now, hand it over or I'll hog-tie you and find it myself."

If he could see her face, he'd see the eat-shit-and-die look he'd come to expect from a complexion and sharp bone structure fit for an angel or a freaking movie star. She snarled and hiked her ass toward him. The tip of a small metal jig protruded from her waistband. He removed it and placed it in his pocket.

A splitting whistle echoed off the concrete columns and walls and ricocheted off the rows of official, and some not so official, vehicles. The four people from his car and three from the other stood at the elevators. Oliver had his foot tapping.

"Yep, still alive." The possibility that she'd used the pick as a lure calmed his cock enough to pass muster. He grabbed her arm. "Let's go. I'm sure Rin would like to get out of the bag pronto."

Tyler escorted her to the elevator and entered his code into the keypad mounted on the wall. Bravo. Uniform. Lima. Lima. Delta. Oscar. Golf. Golf. Echo. Romeo. One. Nine. Nine. Nine. They crammed aboard. No one breathed. Each member of his team hated the idea of bringing such able-

bodied unfriendlies into the building. They
especially hated it since the breach.

The car lifted one level, and the doors opened
to a floor-to-ceiling gleaming onyx foyer. They
stepped into the black box. Behind the one-way
bulletproof glass, the security team for the Base
Branch's Washington, D.C. headquarters hugged
their AKs close, checking the walls of monitors on
their closed circuit system and body scanning the
entire group.

Several hits of this elaborate new system's
low spectrum, "safe" ionizing radiation per day for
the next decade would more than likely mutate his
cells. Maybe he'd develop a superpower. Accelerated
healing would be nice. Lasers out of his eyes might
be cool too. Cancer? Not near as cool but way more
probable. The ridiculous price they paid for safety.

The elevator closed. Cara yanked her arm
from his loosened grip. The collective again held
their breaths. Oliver's blue gaze slid to his in
question, but Tyler called him off. She wouldn't
fight here. It was just her own brand of civil
disobedience. Her shoulder stayed only an inch
from his. Several stilted seconds later, the double
doors to the main entrance swung open.

He signaled the guys ahead of them, smirked,
gripped her upper arm, and followed them down
the corridor to the director's office. Rhonda, the
office mom and director's assistant, held the door
open with a beaming smile. She'd been around long
enough to ignore the black bags on people's heads
and the shackles around their ankles. She'd been
around for too much. His chest itched as if a thread
had come loose on the inside of his shirt, tickling
his skin. Too bad the unraveling thread rooted
deeper.

"Somebody's been to the salon." Hunter leaned to the side, examining the lighter blond locks and sharper cut. "Stunning."

"Well, thank you." Rhonda's cheeks turned a bright shade of pink. She rearranged the locks around her neck, hiding the faint scar.

Tyler looked at his hands. His fingers glistened with her blood. When Oliver also commented on her hair, he blinked away the image. She'd been back to work for three weeks now. How long before the nightmare receded into the background with all the others? Judging by the past, they should have dwindled by now, but this had been different—on their own turf.

Hunter and Oliver filed into the office with their would-be prisoners and settled them into seats in front of Tucker's desk. Tyler stopped in front of the assistant.

"It's good to see you, Rhonda." He painted on a smile.

"Good to be seen." She drew a hand to her neck. "Thank you."

He nodded and pressed forward. What could he say? 'No worries. Pressing my fingers into the side of your neck to stem the flow of your blood was just another day on the job.'

Tucker stood from a simplistic desk chair. The gray at the man's sideburns inched up the hanks of hair, overtaking his close dark crop with increased fervor. In contrast, his eyes no longer resembled New York City road maps. The man also smiled a hell of a lot more these days, which was to say the corners of his mouth shifted north from the perma-neutral he'd seen for the previous five years. While fatherhood would eventually strip his hair of all melanin, domesticity agreed with him. Tucker thanked and excused Rhonda with a nod and motioned for them to remove the restraints and bags.

Time to unleash the beast.

Tyler left her standing. He hoped she appreciated the courtesy enough to leave his balls intact. The bow he'd knotted around her throat loosened with an easy tug. His fingers slipped inside the draw and loosened the string. When he lifted the bag, her gaze shot around the room in a quick calculation of the scene.

Wisps of hair clung to her damp forehead. She ignored them and the collection of moisture on her upper lip. Her blue stare zeroed in on the man behind the desk, effectually dismissing him. Fair enough. His job here was done. Find Cara Lee, the most notorious spy in US history, credited with ripping down the iron curtain and then abruptly disavowed for selling lies. She'd been hunted for generations. With help, he'd found her. That was enough for him. He stepped back and watched Hunter remove the last of the restraints from Damien Luck.

"Thank you, gentlemen. You're dismissed." Tucker directed his gaze at Hunter and Oliver on the other side of the room. So today, everyone ignored him. No skin off his nose. He had a mound of paperwork on his desk, and he had to get his range time in before the end of the week. No doubt they'd be back on the field before then. He stepped into line with the guys, heading out the door. "Tyler, I'd like you to stay."

The Base Branch operatives stalled in the doorway and looked back at Tucker as though he'd lost his ever-loving mind along with the hue of his hair. They always worked together. They were a team, had been since inception. Hunter called them the Uh-Oh Oreos. Now, everyone else did too.

"That'll be all," Tucker said by way of affirmation.

Oliver cleared his throat and continued out the door, shoving Hunter along with him. Tyler took the men's previous place in the back corner. The hairs on his arms stood on end. Good thing no one could see them through his shirt.

Tucker pushed the rolled cuffs of his dress shirt up his forearms. They shifted minimally, stopped by dense muscles. He rounded the desk and offered his hand to Cara. Her gaze rolled up and down him several times before accepting the sturdy, brief shake. Tucker moved on to Damien, who took even longer to accept and then release the hand. That could have been Tucker's reluctance as much as it was Damien's. Last, he stepped in front of Rin. Both Damien and Cara bowed until Tucker knelt in front of the woman.

"I know you're confused and thrilled to have your mother back in your life. I'm going to try my best to make certain she stays there."

Rin nodded but didn't speak. Smart girl.

Tucker stood, stepped to his desk, and hiked a hip onto it. He looked at Cara, who stood ramrod straight. "Please forgive the measures. The secrecy of this facility is more important than your comfort or mine."

"I didn't see you in a black bag." Cara's head tilted.

"I was once. We all were." Tucker shrugged. "I would have approached you on the street, but you wouldn't have believed me."

"You haven't told me anything to believe or not." Her tone was calm, controlled, but the twitch of her hand into a fist gave her away.

"My name is Vail Tucker. I'm the director of the US Office of the Base Branch."

"A myth." Her thin lips formed a sharp line.

"I assure you we aren't." Tucker raised his hand to the office and even Tyler.

"Care to enlighten the less ex-CIA of us in the room? And the less...whatever the hell you guys are?" Damien Luck kicked back in the chair as if he owned the building.

"We're a network of special operations groups for the United Nations located strategically and covertly across the globe to foster peace." Tucker rattled off the mission like it was nothing more than a pitch point. If he went into all the stuff they did, it would be more, a lot more. Too much on most days. Peace came at a cost higher than security.

Cara stepped forward, once again placing herself between the "enemy" and her children. "Your gallantry is endearing. Why am I here?"

"You're clear to stay in the States free from the shadow of your past." Tucker braced his hands on either side of his body and pulled himself more fully onto the desk.

Those pretty pink lips opened and closed. Her jaw worked side to side for a minute. "How?"

"I received evidence of your innocence, dealt with Haskens, and procured your amnesty." Tucker's arms folded loosely over his middle.

Rin leaned forward, grabbed Damien's hand, and squeezed the color from it.

"Why?" Cara hid her excitement better. It hid behind miles and decades of mistreatment. And suddenly, Tyler wanted to know Tucker's reasons as much as she did.

"I want the three of you to work for the Base Branch."

Chapter Three

Rage doused her juvenile excitement in kerosene and lit a match. That was what dreamers got. Burned to a fucking crisp.

Cara turned to Rin, Luck, and Tyler—she liked the name better than Bulldogger. "Excuse us for a moment."

"Grace stays," the director barked.

"Grace?" She pinned him with an I don't give a mother fuck what you want glare.

"Tyler Grace. My operative stays," Tucker insisted. "Damien and Darinda—"

"Please, call me Rin." Her daughter picked one hell of a time to open her mouth. Cara was on the verge of an eruption.

"Rin." Vail Tucker flashed her little girl a wide smile. Why smile when you're trying to relegate someone to a life of horror and hard decisions? "You two may wait outside." He pressed a button on his desk phone.

"Yes, Director Tucker?" Cara recognized the voice over the intercom as his assistant. She wondered what had happened to make Tyler so protective of the woman. He probably hadn't recognized it, but he'd blocked her from Rhonda with his body. Maybe they were together or were about to be.

"Rhonda, please see our guests to the break room." Tucker's hand hovered over the button to disconnect but faltered. "Also, make certain Lieutenant Slaughter is apprised of their arrival."

"Yes, sir," the sweet voice chimed. Cara's voice was never sweet.

The man disconnected and then split his gaze back and forth between them.

"My second in command is in and out packing up her office. She's been known to shoot first and ask questions later, especially after an internal breach. It's fresh in all our minds." Something sad dimmed the light in his eyes. His gaze found Tyler's before returning to her kids. "My assistant was mortally wounded in the attack. So don't give her any shit."

Rin's blue eyes bloated. "We won't."

Luck squeezed her hand and drew her to the door where a middle-aged woman with unnatural but quite pretty blond hair hefted the thing open. Instantly, her estimation between Tyler and the woman changed. The look Rhonda offered him was one of appreciation and not the physical kind. To say nothing of the difference between their ages.

"Right this way." The woman smiled and led them out of the room.

The door hit the frame.

Cara turned to director Tucker. "No."

"You haven't heard the offer," he countered.

"The last government job I had didn't have many benefits," she scoffed.

"We're not the CIA," Tyler interjected from behind her.

"Everyone thinks they're special." She laughed and whipped around to glare at him. "Girls who go to bed with the womanizer. The kid on the honor roll. A soldier going to bat for his country, his beliefs. They're all deluded. So are you. You're just another government organization."

"Not a single government but a network, working together, to advance peace." He stepped forward. "Eliminating any who thwart it."

"You're young. One day, the ideals you believe in will crumble at your feet, and then what?" she challenged.

"I'll fight to get them back." He took another step, bringing his folded arms within reach.

"Our ideals don't crumble," Tucker calmly stated.

"What about your faith in your agents?" Her gaze thinned on Tyler.

"We require proof before we disavow one of our own." Tucker stood, drawing her fixed leer.

"Haskens had proof." She arched a brow.

"No." The director shook his head. "He had hearsay and a static-laced recording with a female voice to hold against a career unparalleled to any before it." He fingered the naked skin on his ring finger and then looked at her.

Cara braced herself for a sad story. He had the look. A little wistful. A little happy. A little sad.

"My fiancée broke into this building and shot me in the gut. That was before I asked her to marry me."

"So you're a masochist?"

"I'm willing to look farther into a situation than the summary page."

"And you're willing to let the bad guy shoot your employees, as long as they're pretty and have a decent reason?"

"My fiancée didn't shoot Rhonda."

"Who did?"

"Her brother."

"Wow. Seems bad decision-making runs in their family. I wouldn't advise procreation."

He smiled. The prideful expression took over his entire face.

"You already did. Is that why you're marrying her?"

"Easy," Tyler warned quietly from far too close.

"You're quite the hypocrite, Cara." Tucker might as well have slapped her cheek.

"Hard-earned life lessons have made me whatever I am." She ignored the tickle in the back of her throat and focused on the swell of belly-churning anger.

"You're judging my fiancée before you know a thing about her, which is what you're afraid our organization will do to you. Carmen broke in the Base Branch to interrogate her brother, Carlos. We had him in lockup for drug and weapons trafficking, among other things. Carlos had kidnapped Carmen's daughter after she refused to go along with the family business plan. He used her daughter's location as leverage to get Carmen on board. When she couldn't beat the information out of him, she did the only other thing she could."

"Shoot you and go along quietly." Cara would do anything for her daughter. Massacre the entire building. That wasn't a great thing, but what right-minded parent wouldn't. A bit of respect for Tucker and his woman rained on her fury. Still.

"I don't want this life for my children." Non-negotiable.

"Damien?" Tucker asked without asking.

"He's mine as much as Rin. I tried to deny that fact because I needed him to help me save her. I put him in danger. I..." She let it trail off. They didn't need to know she hated herself for it.

"I understand," Vail said. "Sophia is mine as much as the child growing inside Carmen is mine. I don't want this life for either of them. They'll probably be as stubborn as my soon-to-be wife and tell me to suck an egg, but that's life."

"I'm past my prime." Cara hated the thought more than she disliked the wrinkles at the corners of her eyes and the deepening crease around her mouth.

"Not even close," Tyler interjected.

"Says the man who flattened me in seconds." Her eyes rolled. She didn't bother to look at him.

"There's not one of us in this place he hasn't gotten the goods on. It's irritating as shit." Tucker scrubbed a hand over his face. "But we all have our strengths. I can out-sleuth him in my sleep." His palms rubbed together. "You're seasoned. I need someone like you to cover my lieutenant commander position."

Cara could never have a "normal" life again. Training turned to instinct far too long ago. This job would give her an honest living, but it would endanger Rin and Luck. She'd made more than her fair share of enemies over the years. Staying would be perfect; everything she'd ever wanted. And it would be so selfish.

"Not interested." She nearly choked on the words.

"Tyler, please leave us," Tucker said.

"Yes, sir." The heat burning into her right shoulder vanished. A small click sounded when the door opened and then closed. Cara swallowed past the tightness in her throat.

Tucker sat in the chair Luck had occupied and offered her the free one she'd never accepted. With a mind full of reservation, she sat. The authority that was his demeanor slipped away, revealing the sad thing he hadn't divulged earlier. Despite herself, her interest piqued. What made this well-established warrior regretful?

"Cara, I know what it is to love someone enough that you think you aren't the best thing for them."

She looked at the ceiling. She counted the slats on the metal grating of a vent in the ductwork.

"That's how she got in." When her gaze returned to Tucker, he continued, "Carmen."

"Oh." Smooth. Words failed her.

"You are what they need."

"No matter the risk?"

"You minimize them, plan for every eventuality, tuck the worry into a small corner of your mind, and live your life...for them and for yourself."

Chapter Four

"Did they bolt as soon as you let them out of the car?" Hunter's fist connected with Tyler's left kidney. Punishing knuckles slid off his slick skin, easing the damage. The words jarred almost as much as the punches. Not that he hadn't pictured Cara shifting into drive, smoking the tires, and leaving trails of rubber on the pavement. He had. Far too often since he pulled away from the curb of the semi-abandoned warehouse, the general shape of her face disrupted the usually streamlined flow of his thoughts. Presently, the basics—a jab, jab, hook or leg bar and flip—would come in damn handy.

"You think she'll run too?" Tyler gritted through the blow to his pride and belly.

"It's all she knows." His sparring partner gritted each word between a succinct series of exploratory punches. Hunter's stacked shoulders flexed and bounded with each relaxed strike, hinting at the devastation they often levied.

She could skip out through Canada in a matter of hours and be on the run again. Living on the run wasn't much different from life during a mission; constantly looking over your shoulder, never knowing what, when, or where things would go to shit. Knowing they would disintegrate the moment you needed them to hold together the most. Though it seemed like it some of the time, he wasn't constantly on a mission. He had friends. He had a house. He had a home with his large, loud family and cows, horses, and space to get away from it all.

Droplets of sweat splattered onto the mat floor, a floor he thought could stand an additional inch of padding. Hunter took the bait, honing in on the gap he'd intentionally left with a lazy front hand. The ominous missile coiled and then shuttled toward his head. Tyler dropped to both knees. He hugged the stocky man's thighs. The image of Rin grabbing her mother assaulted him, a second assailant hiding in the brush.

Hunter's elbow sounded a gong. It reverberated around the various lobes and hemispheres, shattering the treacherous tracks Tyler's steaming brain insisted on traveling. Loose rocks. Neat. Five feet of snow. Wonderful. Yellow tracks. Never better. Full steam ahead. He grimaced, tensed, and straightened his legs. They fell like two lengths of timber.

"Ugh." Oliver grabbed his mid-stage beard and tugged. "I've not seen this manner of suckage since you drank the whole liter of moonshine your daddy gave you to ring in the New Year. If you don't get your shit together, I'm stripping you of your nickname."

Tyler rolled off Hunter, who grabbed his arm, and used the other one to tap three times. "I know. I'm..." The concrete ceiling stared down at him, judging.

"You're intrigued." A hand appeared between him and the ceiling.

"I'm bushwhacked." He didn't take the hand. "We've been teamed up for forever."

"Yeah, our separate assignments have you eating dirt." Hunter's blinding half-smile took the place of his hand. "Right." When the thing went full bore, Tyler squinted.

"Tucker's coming off." Oliver squeaked the words as eagerly as a boy about to hit second base for the first time would.

No way could he blame the guy. They had all been killing time, and each other, to put themselves in the director's path at the end of a long day. Details they'd wanted some hours ago, but international security and little stuff like that came first. Tyler popped off the floor, ignoring the suction of his soaked skin to the plastic. The three of them turned to the right, effectively becoming a barricade to the exit behind them.

A towel hung around the director's shoulders. Sweat rained from the end of his nose, the points of his elbows, and down the center of his too-many pack. Tyler liked beer and cornbread too much to show off every little ab muscle, but that didn't mean they weren't as strong. Tucker dragged the end of the towel over his face and reached for the door. Drops of perspiration splattered against the glass. When he opened the door, the sound of several sets of furious footfalls echoed in the half-mile track's background.

The director strode through the doorway, stepped up to the mat, and pulled the towel off his shoulders. It landed with a splat and a challenge. Tyler breathed, but the man's tilted head stopped him. "All right, boys. First to get me to the mat earns the honor of watching Cara Lee."

Watching Cara Lee? Tyler's brows pinched along with a headache at the center of his forehead. "What makes you think she's still in town?"

"Love for her daughter. Nothing else."
Tucker's head shook. "We, you, have to make sure
she sees us as more than an intergovernmental
strong-arm."

"Me?" Tyler planted a hand on his sopping
chest. His gaze swung left and right. His wingmen
had retreated several steps. "Pussies."

"I like my balls right where they are." Hunter
palmed said appendage in a brief love five of sorts.
"Thank you very much."

Oliver lifted his palms. "I got the stink eye
from Damien and Cara."

"Maybe because you were staring at Rin's and
Cara's legs," Tucker offered.

"I couldn't help myself. I have a thing for
blondes." Oliver shrugged.

Tyler suddenly wished he had sparred Oliver.
He shoved the comment aside and the childish hint
of jealousy. His attention swung to Tucker. "Why
me?"

"You have a way with wild animals. Cara is
essentially a spooked bull." The director's shoulders
bobbed. "I think she could use some gentling."

"We gentle horses, not bulls." Before Tyler got
the words good and out, Tucker came in hard with
hands. Tyler used his mounting angst and his
namesake to pin the director...on the third attempt.
Not bad for fighting a man who'd spent the last
three decades winning all over the world at every
endeavor.

Winning Cara over would be significantly
harder. Even harder still would be to see her on a
daily basis without getting killed or neutered. Of
the two, he'd choose death. Survival meant gentling
her. Quite the paradox, considering he killed people
for a living. He shoved that thought aside in the
heap with Oliver's comment. No time for

psychological analysis. He had to win Cara over, and he knew just the thing to facilitate that. Women liked presents.

Tyler knew the one she'd appreciate most.

Chapter Five

"I can have us out of here, no trace, in one hour." Luck jetted past her into the building's garage.

Cara jerked to a stop at the base of the stairs. The last thing in the world her daughter needed to see was a dead body. Especially today. Especially one Cara had killed. "Upstairs," she ordered.

Luck skidded to a halt and swiveled a wide-eyed questioning look at her.

She offered him a brusque nod and grabbed Rin's hand. Clunking boots and the slap of sandals echoed in the concrete and metal interior. Something shifted inside Cara's chest as she hauled Rin up the steps like a child. As Cara had when she was five and they walked through a congested parking lot, the delicate hand wriggled and jerked against the mandate.

"Do we really need to leave?" Rin planted both feet, forcing Cara to make a decision. Stop or release her daughter's hand. She stopped and turned to find Rin's eyes brimmed with unshed tears. "They said you were free."

"Babe." Luck placed his hand on Rin's shoulder. His thumb rubbed in a sweet circle over the edge of her tank top and bare skin. Her narrow jaw arced toward him. They made such a stunning pair. It wasn't their easy looks but those broken

edges that fit together to make an unparalleled
whole. Even her grudge against the boy couldn't
discount the proof. He kissed the tip of Rin's nose
and then levered back. "People lie."

"Don't I know it." Rin didn't yell the words or
even speak them with anger, which sharpened their
points all the more.

Using fingertips to pinch her sides, Cara
stemmed the flow of blood from the wound her
daughter's truthful words inflicted. She pasted on
the poker face she'd mastered over a lifetime,
turned, and continued. Vail Tucker's proposal had
taken her to her knees almost as much as holding
her daughter again after so many years apart
surely had. His word alone wasn't enough on which
to hang the safety of her daughter and soon-to-be
son-in-law. She needed to cast feelers to her back
alley and high-level informants. Verification of the
Base Branch's existence and Vail Tucker's place in
it would be a starting point. Tyler Grace's would be
icing on the multi-layered cake. But ... if she
verified them, she'd also risk giving away hints on
her location.

Thoughts and ideas fluttered around her like
mayflies over a corpse. If she caught one, another
demanded her attention. She needed to get her
scattered thoughts together. So much had
happened after a decade and a half of nothing.
Nothing but hiding and covering her ass every day
of the year and worrying about her child.

Cara halted on the second landing. Rin and
Luck pulled up short on the small platform with
her. Without thought or preamble, she opened her
arms, closed her eyes, and hoped like hell.

Lanky, lively arms pretzeled her chest, and a
gasp seeped through her lips. She wrapped her
arms around her daughter's back and squeezed the

breath out of them both. Contentment haunted, tugging her heart like a marionette.

She opened an arm, yanked Luck into the fold, and exhaled fully for the first time since they'd left the warehouse. Her head bobbed against Rin's silky hair.

"We're not going anywhere right now," she declared.

"Not leaving?" Luck lurched back. The fight or flight instinct etched his features.

"No. Well, except to get something to eat. Who's hungry?" Cara let her hand squeeze its way down Rin's arm and then around her hand.

"You're not going to take this seriously?" Luck stepped into her path.

"I just got my daughter back. I just got you back. I won't lose either of you by running away from a group who's given me no reason to run and the grace to stay. I will verify Vail Tucker's story and Tyler Grace's background for starters." Unbidden, the use of his name conjured the image of the loose-hipped soldier cowboy. His easy smile and hard hands nabbed her focus. She rubbed a hand over her cheek, enjoying and hating the hint of heat.

"Rin has made a life here." Cara's free hand lifted for Luck's. "You've made a life here and plans for a future." Luck's gaze danced toward the garage and then back. "We won't throw it all away on a whim."

One at a time, they squeezed her hand.

"So where do you want to eat?"

***

"I know what you're doing." Rin pointed her manicured finger at Cara.

"Thank you, Marco." Cara smiled at the boyishly handsome waiter.

"My pleasure." He slid a glass rich with red liquid, bursting with slices of strawberries, oranges, and apples in front of Rin. "Can I get either of you more water?" His gaze slid to Luck's empty chair across from her and next to her daughter's seat.

"That would be lovely." She nodded.

"Any dessert for you this evening?"

"I think we're all stuffed from dinner." Cara's hand instinctively covered her queasy stomach. She'd eaten to soothe Luck's nerves, while she plied her daughter with alcohol to soothe hers.

Mother of the year.

"Can't tell it." The waiter bent at the waist. He winked and flashed Cara a devilish little smile. "I'll be right back with those drinks."

Kids would do anything for a tip these days. Had she been alone on the other side of the world, she might have just let him. She had before. Young men with shaggy hair and foreign accents had saved her soul on more than one occasion.

"Thank you, Marco." She dismissed him with a soft smile.

The waiter hadn't cleared the concrete pedestal and mahogany-topped bar six feet from their table when Rin spouted, "Polo."

Giggles seeped between Rin's punch-red lips. Her hand smacked over her mouth in a futile effort to stem the eruption. The lid had blown and her pent-up emotions—joy, fear, sorrow—spewed out in liquor-soaked laughter.

Cara's hand lifted to her heart. It was the most beautiful sound.

"Another one?" Luck pulled out his chair and sat, his arched brow aimed at Cara. He had excused himself to the bathroom, but from the slight gleam of sweat on his brow, she guessed pretty damn accurately that he'd taken a stroll around the block to check the scene. She didn't offer an explanation, but he knew her motivation. Her daughter had been a tight ball of nerves. When he caught the jingle of Rin's laughter, he forgot about Cara. The corners of his mouth lifted toward the exposed ductwork and lighting. "What?" His question was gentle and bursting with love and curiosity.

Rin doubled over, bracing her forehead against his chest. Maybe they hadn't needed that last drink, after all.

"Polo." Rin wheezed the word out between convulsive snickers.

"Marco. Polo." Luck's head shook back and forth, and slowly, his amusement mingled with hers.

The waiter returned with a pitcher of water and refilled their glasses. It incited an aftershock of laughter, and Marco had good enough sense not to stick around.

Warmth spread from her center and enveloped Cara, save for one cold spot at the base of her neck. This was contentment but not the completion of her mission. She had plenty left to do. Tomorrow.

"Oh, Lord." Rin leaned back and mopped the tears and running mascara from under her eyes. "I don't even like wine."

"Sangria is more fruit than wine." Cara waved a hand in the air, dismissing her worries.

"After three glasses, it's not." Luck pouted.

Cara leaned forward and lifted her glass. Rin lifted hers immediately. After several seconds and a nudge from her daughter, Luck raised his glass. She centered her attention on him first. "Sell the Bentley and buy your food truck." He gave an exaggerated blink, and she turned her gaze on her daughter. "Make wedding plans. I don't know much about them." Cara's marriage to the Russian asshole had been arranged for her. "But I'll be honored to help any way I can." She pressed the cold glass above the table in the center. "To the future."

Chapter Six

Steam rose from the slit in the Styrofoam cup lid on the hood next to him. Only the dim streetlight at the edge of the parking lot allowed him to see it and the rust-riddled railing of the two-story no-tell motel. The moon had slipped off to the other side of the world hours ago, but the sun had yet to make an appearance. Lazy bastard. He enjoyed this time of day more than any other time. Dark didn't mean quiet. Not until the first hours of the morning. The animals, human and non, skirting around civilization in the shadows turned in for the bright day. The law-abiding faction clung to those last precious minutes of sleep. This was the no man's land of time. This was his time.

Tyler gulped the last of his gas station blend and set his empty cup next to the other one. His mouth stretched into a grin. He reached toward the darkness and arched into the ache of his bruised kidney. A growl usually reserved for the side of his bed rumbled to life. When it was over, he deflated slowly, resting his forearms on his knees. Below his cowboy boots, dried exoskeletons and bug guts speckled his chrome bumper.

"Sorry, Talulah. It looks like you won't get that scrub down I promised. Not today, at least." He patted the shiny hood with the edge of his fist. "She's either a late sleeper or she's figured me out.

In which case, we'll be on the road tracking her down for days."

Talulah didn't respond. His 2500 never did. It was what he liked best about her. Well, that and her ability to tow over a dozen head of cattle.

A soft click echoed around the corner, followed by the easy tread of small shoes. Heeled shoes. Chalk up a win for the good guys.

Cara Lee rounded the corner heading for the bus stop, he'd guessed. She didn't have a car. Not that she couldn't jack one in a few seconds or rent one, but last night at ten p.m., he'd followed Rin Lee's Accord to this out of the way spot. He watched Luck see Cara inside and then tour the exterior, looking for him or someone like him. Too bad for the guy, Tyler was staked out two blocks away on the roof of an old bank.

The fraction of a second before she noticed him perched on the hood of his truck made the sleepless night an easy price to pay. Half-mast eyes surveyed the area with insipid interest. While she'd run for many years, not being caught inflated her confidence. Elegant legs glided over the cracked sidewalk in low-slung stilettos with a nonchalance that had him thinking of an afternoon of unhurried, sweaty entanglement.

Sleepy eyes snapped to attention. Every languid muscle contracted, drawing her up taut as a rope towing a ton. Cheekbones meant for a muse pointed at him rife with accusation.

"How the hell did you know where I was staying?" Her voice shook.

"Morning." Tyler slid from the front of Talulah and regretted it the moment he was airborne. Coiling his knees to absorb the landing only added to the reverberation up his back. Hunter had done a number on him, and it was all this lady's fault.

"Don't try and sweet talk me. How did you know where I was staying?"

"Sweet talk? Darlin', I haven't started sweet talking you. When I do, trust me, you'll know." He reached back, pulled both coffee cups off Talulah, and offered the fresh one to Cara.

She dodged him and stomped away.

He caught up with her and kept stride before they passed the next motel room door.

"How'd you know?" she snarled.

"Do you think I cop a feel on all the steer I wrestle?"

Pianist fingers immediately combed through her hairline and then roamed over her collarbone, searching for the paper-thin tracking device. They reached the road in short order. She forced her hands to her sides. "Well, you are from the South."

"Ouch!" Tyler tossed his empty cup into the garbage outside the bus portico and then clutched his heart. "Low blow. I may have to take my coffee back."

"I haven't taken your coffee." Her arms flew out from her sides.

"But you will." He winked.

"Pfft. You wish."

He shrugged. "It's not poisoned."

"It'd be the first."

"That rough, huh?"

She shoved her hands into her pockets and stared at the steaming cup. A grin niggled, but he kept it locked down. Her light blue gaze found his. "You have no idea."

"No, I don't suppose I do." The sincerity in her expression sucker punched him. "Want to tell me about it?"

"Hit up the local library. I'm sure they have a story time." She turned away. The back of her head was as pretty as the front. Hair piled atop her head in a tight bun showed off the fine curve of her neck.

"They don't tell your story."

Her head snapped in his direction. "And neither do I. Why are you here?"

"Nate Harlow wasn't in your roundup yesterday. I'll guess he's your first stop this morning." Besides the Base Branch, which was an unknown she was surely trying to figure out, her daughter's ex-lover/CIA operative was the enemy she'd surfaced to handle. No way would she leave that stone unturned.

"Shows what you know." Her brows danced.

Was she bluffing or did she have other business this morning? He couldn't tell. "Oh, really?"

"I'm not your concern."

"Actually." He smiled because she was the best mission he'd had in years. "You are. If you start killing people willy-nilly, Base Branch won't be able to sanction your amnesty."

"You need a body to prove death, much less murder." Thin lips outlined white teeth. Her lower incisor was shifted back and to the side, just a little, giving her mystery more depth.

"Nate knows that, which is why he went dark after his handler vanished."

"He won't be hard to find."

"Not at all." Tyler held out the Styrofoam cup. "Take a ride with me?"

Chapter Seven

Interstate turned to highway and quickly
devolved to a narrow, pitted excuse for a road that
still boasted a highway sign. Cara slammed the cup
of coffee she'd polished off many miles and minutes
ago into the console's holder. She yanked the seat
belt from her neck and glared at Tyler Grace.
"Where are you taking me?"

"Anticipation is half the fun."

"I don't like surprises."

"Then you haven't had the right ones." He
slid her a salacious casual glance and then took it
away before she could berate him for it or even be
certain it wasn't just her imagination running
amok.

Cara tossed herself against the seat like a
child. The seat belt choked her for the offense.
"Shit. Is this thing made for giants?" She grabbed
the material and held it off her irritated skin.

The right front tire drifted off the edge of the
road. Her brains bumped and lurched with the
uneven ground. "What..." Her grip tightened on the
seat belt, and her other hand joined in as the truck
rolled to a stop on a steep hill.

Tyler unbuckled.

Cara's brain didn't scream as it should have.
The hairs on the back of her neck neglected to
stand on end. Her heart revved. That little spin of

adrenaline was the extent of her reaction.
Regardless, she lunged for the gun at her ankle.

"Well, that just proves it," he drawled.

Cold hard metal greeted her palm. Her hand
wrapped around the butt of her pistol, but his tone
more than his words gave her pause. She kept her
hold but looked across the cab. "Proves what?"

"That you like wrestling with me." He drew
his bottom lip into his mouth and pulled it out with
a sweet smile.

"It proves I don't trust you."

"Maybe. Maybe it proves you don't trust
yourself. Because you know I won't hurt you." His
elbow rested on the center console. The confines of
his worn, gray T-shirt showcased his shoulders and
the serrated edge of his obliques. He moved slowly
and steadily, closing the space.

Cara's throat constricted. She released the
handle and planted her back against the door and
cool window. His face hovered a foot and half away
from hers, yet the proximity pulled heat to her
cheeks. Other places too. His thickly corded
forearm reached out past her head to a knob on the
wall panel.

"I wish you'd said something forty minutes
ago." He adjusted the seat belt to the lowest setting.
"Your neck is red." His gaze stroked over the spot as
surely as a caress.

Her hand flew to the light abrasion. "It's fine."

"Mmm." Tyler withdrew back to his seat,
buckled, and checked the rearview mirror before
pulling onto the road.

Mmm. What the hell did that mean? It didn't
matter. Cara scrubbed a hand down her face and
situated in her seat. The belt fit neatly between her
breasts and over her shoulder. She should've
thought of it. Better yet, she should have stuck to

her no. Annoyed with herself as much as Tyler, she turned toward the window while they coasted over gradually rising and tapering hills.

Hues of yellow and pink tickled the horizon, giving life to the day and shape to the former darkness outside. Lush foothills reached toward the sky, one outdoing the other as they stretched north and east. As the sun rose, it colored the cotton-clouded horizon in shades of pink. It contrasted with the green grass and trees, while wooden fences outlined manmade boundaries for miles in every direction.

Minutes later, Tyler turned onto a gravel drive lined with large oaks. It wound over a small creek and split large fields speckled with horses. If he'd brought her horseback riding, she'd shoot him for certain. She didn't have time for moony shit. Though she'd enjoyed the sport once upon a time.

Trees opened to a two-story white brick farmhouse wreathed with a garden and archway bursting with blooms. The drive split, offering a circular path in front of the ethereal home and a path around back. Gardens and grass sprawled for acres, creating the feel of an old English country estate. Tyler drove around the house and parked under a white pergola bowed with the weight of the greenery it hosted. He turned off the engine and hopped out of the truck that had taken well-placed foot and handholds for her to climb inside.

In front of her sat an understated stone patio, leading to a red back door. The vibrant color matched the large red barn 100 yards from the house. Her door opened, filling the cab with morning light. Gardenia blossoms scented the air that filtered in with it, overtaking the new car scent with nature. She filled her lungs.

"Heaven, isn't it?" Tyler stood in the yawning gap between her and the ground and offered his hand.

Cara nipped her burgeoning smile. "I'm not getting out until you tell me what this place is. Do you live here?"

"Sometimes." He shaded his eyes from the bright rays and looked up at her like, 'What's the big deal?'

"How the hell can you afford this place?" No way could he afford this on a Base Branch salary. The CIA hadn't paid her enough to cover the driveway. No governmental agency would. Give us your blood, firstborn, your life. Oh, here's a pittance for your trouble. But we pay leaders—the talking heads—enough to buy small countries. Bureaucracy at its finest.

"I didn't say I owned it." His smile caught the rays and blinded her.

"You haven't said much of anything."

Again, he offered his hand and that disarming, lopsided grin. Cara glared. A curl of dark hair peeked out the collar of his shirt at the base of his neck between the carved parameter of his pectorals.

"It belongs to the Sanfords, my parents' business partners and good friends."

Oh, God. She lusted over a guy who lived with his parents' friends. Wasn't that worse than living with his parents?

Cara jerked her gaze to his. "What business are your parents into?"

"Cattle. The Sanfords have the best horses."

"Where are they?"

"In the pasture. You didn't see them in the field on the way in?" Again with the winking.

"The Sanfords, smartass."

"Somewhere in the Mediterranean. They travel a lot. So do I. It helps them to have someone to oversee their business while they're gone, and it gives me a break from..." His gaze slid to the side and then back. "Well, you know."

She did—too well. "Why are we here?"

"Get out and find out." He took a step back, throwing down the gauntlet.

Never one to back away from a challenge, Cara slid off the seat. It was a long way to the ground, and she landed in a crouch. When she stood, Tyler's chest was too close. "You know this thing is hell on gas and the environment. It's not too kind to knees either." Jesus. She sounded so old. And she was too old to do this flirty thing. *Stick to business, Lee.*

He hitched his scrawled silver belt buckle. His very large belt buckle. "Yep, it is. But it hauls horse flesh a mite better than a Prius."

This guy kept her off balance, a shitty thing while she navigated a tightrope with her daughter in one hand and her adopted son in the other. Cara cleared her throat and ducked around Tyler. She hurried across the stone path toward the house but didn't know where to go. Her steps faltered a few feet from a cast iron fire pit. "Where to?"

"The barn."

"I didn't come out of hiding to pet a horse."

The massive structure loomed larger than any barn she'd ever been inside. Not that she'd been inside many. She changed course and rushed toward it, ready to have this surprise unveiled. He caught up and matched her hurried steps easily.

"How about a bull?" His brows waggled.

Before she could stop herself, she found his gaze and rolled her eyes, feeding his mischief. A deep boom of laughter radiated from his drum

chest and thick throat. The honest smile tugged at
his cheeks, forming lines around his squinted eyes.
The muscles in his neck striated, and his face
lifted.

Cara's heartbeat wobbled at the rich sound.
Shit. She practically sprinted to the barn and
levered one end of the large post barring the
massive double doors.

"Psst."

She ignored him, worked her hands toward
the middle and lifting the other side from the
latch...just not quite enough.

"Cara Lee." He said her name like an
admonishment. Like he could order her around.
Her back stiffened. No, sir. She wasn't any man's
possession. No man would ever again order her
around.

Muscles bunched and feet planted, Cara
heaved the board out of both latches and across the
stretch of gravel in front of the barn. Her chest
puffed. She turned to face Tyler.

That damn smirk said it all. The smirk and
the cool way he propped his wrist on the top of the
small open door cut out of the far corner of the
barn.

"Mother fuck." Her scowl shifted between him
and the length of wood laid like a fallen soldier on
the grass.

"Go ahead. I'll wait." One stitched boot
crossed over the other, point down. "It was
impressive." The thumb on his free hand hooked
into the front loop of his jeans.

The aroma of flower petals mixed with
manure filled and exited her lungs in rapid
succession. Her fingers balled, and she let them.
She wanted to throttle him, but she'd learned her
lesson the first time. With no other options besides

shooting him, she stomped to the board and used her exacerbation to lift it and reposition it in the latches.

Dirt clung to her palms, so she rubbed them together. Specks of sand rolled from one spot to another on her damp skin without falling off. No way was she wiping them on her gray sleeveless top. Instead, she opted for the back of her high-waisted jeans. Shit, again. Their outfits almost matched, save for the hick factor.

Cara pulled a long, calming breath and headed for the small, easy door.

"I didn't figure you as one for flowers or chocolates. So..." He unhooked his thumb from the loop and gestured toward the interior.

Hesitantly, she walked through the opening into the abyss. Pitch darkness clung to every corner of the building, but in the center, a spotlight bathed Nate Harlow's naked form. His arms stretched over his head, bound by a knotted rope and secured to the beam running the length of the barn. Sweat slicked his skin and matted his hair to his head.

Cara looked at Tyler. This guy kept the surprises coming.

"He's all yours." He nodded at Nate. "Just remember what I said earlier."

Chapter Eight

Tyler pulled the door closed behind him, shrouding the corner in darkness.

The rope squeaked against the rafter with each jerk of Harlow's head. He bobbed it left and right, trying futilely to see what monster stalked him in a wide circle.

Cara shed her irritation with him and slipped into her new role of tormentor as easily as he imagined she'd slip out of the sexy, conservative number she wore and into a pretty negligee. Not for him, of course. She held him at arm's length and wished her arms were longer. That was fine. He affected her. He'd started the parry as a means of distraction. Now? The more he touched her, the more he wanted to touch her.

Not a great move. Especially with a woman of Cara Lee's caliber.

A few feet per orbit, she neared, taunting the man.

Harlow set his jaw and wrinkled his forehead, acting hard. It hadn't taken Tyler much effort to overtake him, and Harlow had been unconscious when he'd left him to retrieve Cara. He'd come to in a spotlight, surrounded by darkness.

She stepped into the pouring light wearing a devilish version of the smirk he'd seen on her lips a few times before.

Harlow bit his lips. Desperate measures to keep his shit together. Tyler propped a hip on a stacked heap of square bales and folded his arms over his middle. Spiky heels led Cara's prowl. Each strike of the point to the concrete isle elicited an involuntary quiver in Harlow's middle. His stiff jaw slacked.

After one close circle, Cara stopped in front of Harlow and turned the side of her face to Tyler. "If I'd known you had him, I'd have brought my tools." She waved a hand in the air. "No matter. We're in a barn with plenty of useful devices for the job."

"Popov will kill you for this." Harlow bared his teeth and flexed the heavy muscles covering his short skeleton.

Cara giggled. The sound skated up Tyler's spine, and he wasn't the one at her mercy. "It's cute you think she gave a shit about you. Really, it is." She strolled off the concrete. Her heels sank into the mixture of hay, dried manure, pine bedding, and dirt.

Dusty saddles, bridles, and ropes occupied one-half of the wall adjacent to the makeshift torture chamber. The other half was reserved for farming tools. Axes, spades, rakes, machetes, and pitchforks. Several hollowed wood eyes in the wall added to the barn's eerie feel. Cara grabbed the longest pitchfork, the one with six closely spaced tines.

"It's even cuter," she said, returning to her prey, "that you think she could get the upper hand. Especially since she's at the bottom of the Potomac."

"Fucking bitch." Rage colored Harlow's cheeks.

Tyler hadn't been the only one busy last night. If it was true. The solid lump in his stomach said this lady didn't bluff.

Cara strolled forward into Harlow's strike zone. The lump in his belly coated with lead, and he dug his heels into the ground to keep from intervening. She knew what she was doing.

"At the bottom of the Potomac...where I put her." Her eyes glinted with inciting mischief.

Harlow wrapped his hands around the rope above his arms. His legs snapped into the air. One calf hooked the back of Cara's neck. The other shin smashed the front of her throat, compressing her windpipe.

A bale flew off the stack. Tyler reached the outer halo of light in a blink. That was when he saw her hand in a flat palm, facing him, telling him to stop.

Right.

A wrapped breath wheezed from her compressed throat. He ground his heels into the dirt to stay put.

Another rasp filled the darkness. "Let's see how long you can hold up all those bulky muscles."

"Longer than you can hold your breath."

Cara wedged the pitchfork between Harlow's nuts and the concrete, fork up. "If I can breathe enough to talk, I can hang..."

The muscles in Harlow's legs contracted.

"...all day." Her reedy voice contradicted the statement. Then again, with those tines pressed against his sack, Harlow's skin collected moisture like a leaf in the rainforest.

Each tick of the hands on Tyler's watch offended him while Cara's neck remained trapped. Thirty seconds. Sixty. Seventy. A bead of sweat rolled down Tyler's arm.

The rope hanging from the rafters lurched and vibrated. Harlow's muscles twitched, causing the sway. Cara chuckled. The twitches turned to convulsions. Collected sweat poured off his body. Large drops landed on the tips of Cara's shoes and arms.

"I give. I give." Harlow released her throat and hinged his legs on her back, desperate to keep himself off the tines. "Get this thing off me!"

Cara's lips moved, but no sound followed. She coughed, swallowed, and tried again. "Let me do it my way."

She wasn't looking at him, but Tyler knew she was talking to him. He also knew exactly what she wanted permission to do. His insides clenched. An affirmative and she'd slit Nate's throat. Even a hint of hesitation and she'd eliminate the threat.

"What way?" Nate screeched.

"No. We already talked about this."

"Fine. I need you to make me a promise, Nate."

"What?" He screamed the word.

"No grudges. No vendettas. Nothing involving me and especially my daughter."

"Fine! Fine!" His head shook. Sweat slung.

"I need better than fine."

"I won't bother you, either of you." His voice raised with each syllable.

"Ever," Cara clarified.

"Not ever." Harlow agreed to a plea.

"If you do..." Cara grabbed the pitchfork's handle and gave it a tug. Harlow howled. "You'll wish I'd ended you today."

"I hear you." Harlow's lips etched in pain. "Now, move the damn thing, please."

"Nice talk, Nate. I never want to see you or your sweaty balls ever again."

Cara kicked the bottom of the wooden handle, releasing Harlow from his nutcracker. His legs slipped off the side of Cara's shoulders and landed on the concrete with a slap. Done with him, Cara collected the pitchfork, sauntered to the wall, and replaced her tool.

Tyler walked around the shadows and approached the man from the back. He lifted the black bag from the ground where he'd left it and roped Harlow with the fabric. The captive's soaked head bobbed left and right, leaving dark pools of moisture on the bag.

"When can I leave?"

After crafting a knot that ensured the bastard wouldn't see his face, he strode toward the door. Cara met him at the small opening and ducked through it without a backward glance at Nate Harlow.

"You hungry?" He closed the door, locked it, and then placed a hand on the small of her back.

"I need to get back to the city." Her voice sounded like she'd eaten glass for breakfast.

She needed some water and some honey, but he didn't say it. "Big plans for the day?"

"I can skip penance, since you're a saint and wouldn't let me sin. I won't need a shower, either, since I have not even a speck of blood on my hands."

"Today," he amended.

She shrugged and headed for his truck. "I need to find the tracker you put on me, and then, if your boss was serious—"

"He was."

"I'm taking my daughter house shopping."

"Give me just a second and we'll head out."

Tyler unlocked the house, dipped into the kitchen, and grabbed some bottled waters from the fridge and a honey throat lozenge Mrs. Sanford kept in a cabinet above the sink. By the time he returned to the truck, Cara sat strapped into the passenger seat pinning her lopsided bun and looking more regal than anything Talulah had ever hauled. He hopped in, laid his offerings on the center console, and pulled down the beautiful drive before the sun crested the tree-covered mountains.

"Thanks."

He didn't know exactly what she thanked him for, but she twisted a top off one of the water bottles and guzzled half in three long pulls. The back of her hand doubled as a napkin after she polished off the rest. Ladylike with a twist. He opened one of the other bottles and took a few swigs.

"I haven't had that much fun with a naked man in a long time." She sighed.

Water revolted, working its way up Tyler's nose and out his mouth. It stung. He sputtered and hacked. "If that's not an incentive to keep my clothes on, I don't know what is."

Her head shook and her lips folded around the bite of her teeth in an effort not to smile.

"What? You don't want me to keep my clothes on?" he asked, recapping his bottle and setting it in the door pocket.

Thin lips escaped and spread into a shallow grin. "When are you going to take him back?"

"Sly subject change." Tyler pulled onto the skinny highway. "I'm not."

"What about your no kill speech?" Her mouth formed a pout.

"I'm just sending him in the opposite direction of your daughter with a tracker that will let me know if he ever breaks our deal."

"I didn't need you to find him for me."

Tyler wondered how long it would take such an independent woman to get her back up about a little assistance. One mile. He'd have bet on less. His grip doubled on the steering wheel, anticipating her wrath. "I know you didn't. It was a peace offering."

"Like flowers or chocolates?" When he ventured a glance in her direction, one brow curved in an artistic arch.

"Conventional." He shrugged. "It's boring."

She gave a slight nod, and then the dam broke on her smile. This wasn't sinister like the one he'd seen in the barn. It wasn't sarcastic or vindictive like the ones she'd offered him so many times in the last twenty hours. It wasn't motherly and endearing like the ones she'd aimed at Rin and Luck.

Severe cheeks formed rounds as tight as racquetballs. Deep grooves curved on either side of her mouth, which stretched wide, revealing rows of straight white teeth—save for that crooked little incisor. Elusive and unadulterated joy revealed a dim, beautiful light at Cara's center.

It warmed him from the inside out.

"Thank you," she whispered.

His inner warmth faltered. In a few days, she wouldn't be thanking him.

Chapter Nine

It wasn't a lie exactly. They house hunted. Only, a day later. She'd needed time to tend to business, and Rin had needed time with Luck to... Nope. Her mind didn't need to travel that road. Not where her daughter was concerned. It had plenty of side streets, back alleys, and roundabouts of its own.

"So what do you think about the block?" Rin leaned over the table, grabbed her cup, and sucked the dregs from some iced mocha thing.

Nobody drank straight coffee anymore. One guy did, but she'd forbidden herself to think about Tyler Grace. Naturally, she shoved open the shop door, stepped onto the hot sidewalk, and surveyed the length of the neighborhood street for him.

Since he'd air dropped her from the side of his sky-scraping truck yesterday, she hadn't seen him. It didn't mean he wasn't surveilling from a distance, but she hadn't felt the niggle at the base of her skull like she usually did when someone watched her. He was probably recouping from a long night hiding Nate so she wouldn't kill the asshole.

"It's busy." Cara dodged a clump of strollers and moms in yoga pants in a dead heat for the aroma of sugar and coffee beans. "If you don't mind

the constant coming and going, it's nice. I wonder
what it's like at night?"

"Another hour and we'll find out." Rin struck
out at an upbeat pace full of energy for the hunt,
even after a full day of work.

"How far away is the restaurant where we're
meeting Luck?"

"It's a few blocks past the last of the houses
on my list. I mapped it out on my lunch break."

"Do you ever relax? Take a minute for
yourself?"

"Sure, I do. I just haven't. Not since things
went crazy in a yay-my-mom's-not-really-dead sort
of way." Her daughter turned her face to the waning
sun, soaking up its light.

Rin was light. Despite everything. Despite
her.

Cara was the darkness. The same day she'd
used her daughter as bait and spent the night
planning a future with her and her fiancé—i.e.
house hunting to rid Rin of the infected home she'd
shared with Nate Harlow—Cara set off into the
shadows to tidy up her mess. The mess being the
body she'd stuffed into the trunk of one of the cars
in Luck's garage. She replayed the memory,
watching as Popov's bullet-riddled corpse bobbed
like a cork. Pulled by the weights, her legs
submerged. Her crooked torso and arms followed.
Until finally, her dour face sank beneath the
rushing black water.

"Mom?"

She hadn't heard the term applied to her in
so long that her breath caught. "Yes?" she rasped.

"I asked cottage house, condo, or full
outhouse, house?"

Great. Now that she was finally present, she
was absent.

"It depends. How long do you plan to stay there? If you're looking at a couple of years, a condo or cottage like you have now would do just fine. Anything longer and you might want a yard for a dog? Kids? If you'd want those things."

Rin's brows sank. Her fingers picked at a clump of frayed fabric at the end of her cutoffs. "I don't know." She adjusted the strap of her purse and then hugged her arms around her stomach. "We haven't talked about those things. It's all happened so fast."

Her daughter's blue eyes flitted about, and an absent grin tugged at her mouth. "It feels right," she said almost to herself. Those brilliant eyes lifted to Cara's. "More right than anything has felt before, but is it too fast?"

"I'm certainly not the one to ask about matters of the heart."

Cara had only ever truly loved one person, and look what she'd done to her. She'd abandoned her. She'd missed Rin's first kiss, her first period, the deliberation about what she'd do with the rest of her life, walking across the stage at graduation, boy troubles, resumes, jobs. So damn much.

"But," she added when the light in Rin's eyes dimmed, "instinct is an invaluable trait. If this feels different, that tells you something. Were your other relationships..." Son of a bitch. Cara hadn't maintained any kind of relationship over the past two decades. Not a single friendship to speak of. She didn't know how to voice her thoughts.

"They were convenient and uninspiring," Rin offered.

"Luck is nothing close to convenient." Cara's head shook. "But he is enlivening. He's loyal. He's loving."

Rin nodded. Her shoulders straightened, and the upbeat tempo of her steps returned. "How'd you meet him?"

"The little shit tried to fleece me in Rio and got more than he bargained for." They strolled. "He was a cocky teenager, determined to prove himself in a street gang. Most of them were poor but not alone. They could have chosen a different path. School. A trade. Luck's mother had abandoned him." A searing pain lanced Cara's heart. "He had no one and no options. He stole to feed himself."

Her daughter's wide eyes drank in every word.

"I couldn't help you without placing you in danger, but I could help him. As much as I saved him, taught him, he saved me more. I was in a dark place."

"You were alone too," Rin whispered.

"I don't mind solitude. I've grown quite fond of it over the years."

"Then what?"

"It was you. I couldn't bear another minute away from you, no matter what. I'd decided to take you, to steal you away from everything and everyone you'd ever known, so I could be your mother again. I knew it was reckless and so damn selfish, but I couldn't stop myself. I'd made plans, paid for new papers. The entire time I knew I shouldn't, but I would have."

They'd stopped on the sidewalk close to the storefront. Rin stared at her as if she'd grown snakes for hair. "Why didn't you?"

"I met Luck." Cara blinked away collecting moisture and pressed on. There was no way to know how many days, hours, minutes they'd have together. Her daughter had a right to know everything. "I saw the rage he had for his mother, and I was terrified."

"You were scared I'd reject you." Rin swatted at a stray tear. "Okay." Her head bobbed in a furious beat.

Cara's insides twisted.

"Okay," Rin said again with both palms up. "I think I've had enough for today."

"Okay." The skeleton, muscles, and ligaments holding Cara together fractured. She stumbled back a step.

"No, I don't mean I want you to leave. I just. I can only take these stories in little doses. It's so much to wrap my head around." She cupped the sides of Cara's face. "I want to hear it. I need to hear it. And I want you to stay. In fact, since I don't know what to look at for Luck and me, I have a few apartments and condos in the area we could look at for you." Her daughter swatted several windblown strands from her face and forced a smile.

She'd missed that smile, watching it morph through the years. The weight that had lifted yesterday returned with a vengeance and extra pounds. She'd missed the thousands of times her daughter's hand had reached for her...and she hadn't been there.

Sweat clung to Cara's upper lip. The niggle leapfrogged to full-on gnawing of her cerebellum. She grabbed Rin's hand and yanked them into a narrow alley at the end of the block between the row of shops and the first clump of townhomes. Cara herded her daughter past the beer cans and cigarette butts toward the outlet at the back of the shops. Inside her chest, her heart raced ahead as if she was in a marathon. The alley walls wavered. Her steps faltered.

"Hold up."

Rin grabbed her elbow with her free hand and guided her to the brick wall. They were exposed. They had to run.

"Head between your knees." Rin shoved her head down.

Cara tensed to protest, but suddenly, upside down, the world stopped vibrating.

"If you're not ready to look for a place, all you have to do is say. No panic attack necessary."

Panic attack? Cara placed her hands on the knees of her navy slacks, but the sweaty palms slipped off. She settled for her elbow and dragged one breath after another into her lungs. Jesus. She couldn't pick an apartment or a townhouse. She couldn't move forward because every time she looked into her daughter's brilliant blue eyes, joy and sorrow crushed her soul.

That stunning face popped into her field of vision tilted at an odd angle. "That better?" Cara's back slid down the wall, bringing her to a crouch. Rin straightened. "There's a park less than a block from here. Why don't we go sit and people watch?"

"Stop!" The demand flew from Cara's shaky lips.

"Stop what?" Her daughter gave as good as she got.

"Being so nice to me. I abandoned you. I don't..." Her voice cracked. "I don't deserve your smiling face and concern. I know you're angry. I'm angry." A hiccupped sob stopped her tirade.

Rin crouched in front of her and leveled their gazes. "I wasted my teenage years being mad. I would smash a rock through a car window just to watch it shatter. I'd set things on fire and relish in the destruction. I'd get into fights to forget, for one minute, how much I hurt."

Cara looked away. Tears streamed down her cheeks.

"I was so angry I missed my youth and nearly destroyed my future." Rin wrapped her hand around Cara's wrist. "Anger won't make me better. It won't make you better either." She met her daughter's gaze. "I can't imagine what you went through, what leaving a child would do to someone." She couldn't take it. Her gaze dropped to the dirt, but Rin pulled her chin up. "Even if it was for my own good. We've both suffered. Now, it's time to heal."

But how? Killing Popov hadn't helped much. Reconciling with Rin was a start, but the weight still compressed her insides.

Chapter Ten

Tyler's knuckles hovered over the flimsy door, ready to knock again when a loud metal click and thunk jarred the thing to life. It groaned open. Cara stood in the gap with a sheet pinned haphazardly over the soft mounds of her breasts and a spit-shined pistol aimed at his chest. Gone was the prim hardass, and in her place was a disheveled, vulnerable woman.

"Shit." She moaned louder than the door. The barrel of her gun lowered to the ground. One hand held the gun and front of the crumpled sheet, while the other hiked an end and wound it around herself.

"Morning." He tipped his imaginary hat.

Red camouflaged the whites of Cara's eyes, rimming the striking blue with despair. Still, she glared, showing a bit of that hot, cynical, tear-him-a-new-one-as-soon-as-I-kiss-him demeanor he'd come to expect. Her gaze lowered to the coffee in his left hand and the paper sack in his right.

"Coffee and breakfast? What do you want now, a kidney?"

"Nah, I'd settle for a peek under your sheet."

"I have a weapon." She waggled the tip of the pistol.

"Darlin', from where I'm standing, you *are* a weapon."

A snorted groan accompanied her eye roll. She turned into the room, leaving him in the open doorway. Tyler took the indifferent invitation and stepped inside. Stale air—the prepackaged, overused kind—assaulted his nostrils. He left the door open for several beats, hoping it would help circulate some oxygen. Also, it was the only source of light in the room.

The comforter lay in a heap on the floor at the end of the king-size bed next to a pile of navy slacks and white shirt. Lace panties and a sheer bra topped the heap like whipped cream. A duffle bag lay on the counter at the far end of the room with its contents spilling out on either side. Near the sink, a tube of toothpaste had lost its cap among the toothbrush, assorted compacts, and mascara.

Cara sat in an armchair beside the nightstand, traded the pistol for a small signature white and red box, and drew her feet into the seat. Haunted eyes stared ahead at a blank television screen and flipped up the lid. She tipped the pack and extricated a cheap red lighter. After closing the pack and wedging the plastic height between the index and middle finger on her right hand, she opened and closed the package again and again.

Tyler closed the door, plunging the room into darkness for twenty stilted seconds, while his eyes adjusted to the faint shafts of light seeping in through the heavy curtain. In a sad melody, Cara continued to open and close the box. Two short steps brought him to a small round table. When he dropped the bag, it crashed like a cymbal in her pitiful tune. The cup thumped. He grabbed one of the two chairs from under the table. It smacked down in front of the armchair, sparking her ire. She stopped the incessant beat and kicked her bare legs onto the floor.

"I didn't peg you for a smoker or a slob." He straddled her legs and sat.

Cara donated a hollow laugh. "They belonged to my husband."

"Rosik Idlen?" Surprise and something else translated into a clipped tone.

"The very one."

"He was Russian."

She offered a flat-line stare in return.

"Marlboros?"

Her gaze raked from his boot to belt buckle and back. The chant, 'Don't pop wood,' played round and round in his brain. It didn't help. The thought of Cara married to the miserable excuse for a human did.

"He had a secret obsession with cowboys, always smoked these in the privacy of his home study and watched old Westerns whenever the help had gone home for the day."

She hadn't said their home.

"I didn't know you married him." He also didn't know why it mattered one way or the other.

"How else do you think I got him to support Gorbachev and let me sneak into his files? A mistress holds a man's cock, but a wife holds his ear and those of his friends. Even if he thinks her inferior." She smiled with vacant eyes. "It actually helps."

An insidious vision of Cara under the heel of the potbellied asshole chilled his blood. "Why keep them?"

Her gaze livened at his growl. She shoved the lighter inside the pack and set them on the nightstand. Long fingers cocooned the small box as though they protected a baby bird from a raccoon. Her hand stayed outstretched, but she leaned forward aligning their eyes.

"Actions and reactions," she breathed.

"Care to explain?" Her musky scent overtook the staleness, spiking his brain with pheromones. The chill vanished, replaced with a warmth similar to a three finger shot of whiskey.

"You first. Why are you here?"

"Nate headed west. He has family in Chicago."

He studied her thick brows and the proud ridge of her petite nose. Dark circles shadowed her eyes. The steep rise of her forehead curved gracefully around her hairline to the sharp edge of her jaw.

"That's it?" Her fingers slid from the pack and gripped the front of the sheet. Haughtiness returned, drawing her mouth into a calm pout.

"Not even close." Tyler leaned forward, narrowing the gap between their mouths. The pulse bumped in her long column neck, but otherwise, she remained perfectly still. Blond hairs kinked from sleep lounged along her shoulders. A damp curl nestled in the hollow of her collarbone.

"Tyler?" Her breath warmed his lips.

"Mmm?"

"You know I'm old enough to be your mother."

His gaze continued down the slope of her shoulders, down the taut muscles of her arms. He swallowed the excess saliva pooling in his mouth and met her gaze.

"Not even close."

Her jaw twitched. "My daughter is more your demographic."

"Is she now?" His head tilted, and he eased ever slightly closer.

Cara closed the gap between them. Her nose coasted up the edge of his cheek. His eyes closed, committing the caress to memory.

"She is." Her words danced between his stubble and coasted into his ear.

"Good to know." He opened his eyes and turned them on her in challenge. Their gazes held heartbeat upon heartbeat.

Her lips parted. She flicked her tongue across her back teeth and then stood. The white sheet grazed his nose from her breasts, across her abdomen, and to her belly. Blood rushed to the farthest reaches of his body, draining away his intelligence. He'd plunge headfirst and ask questions later. She drew him in. Her sorrow. Her body. Her branded soul.

"It's too bad she's taken." Cara stepped around his legs and was gone.

Tyler forced his head to stay upright when all he wanted to do was let it hang. His skin tingled. His hands shook. He forced the reaction down.

"Rin and Luck are moving in together, just as soon as they agree on a place." He turned to find her hand on the door. She twisted the knob and jerked it open. "So you'll have to look elsewhere for entertainment."

"I'm not looking for entertainment, Cara."

"What are you looking for?"

"Not a damn thing." It was just too fucking bad he'd found it anyway.

He'd looked for years, needing something to fill the patchwork of holes every kill left in his heart. Most of his comrades could lay waste to the enemy without a second thought. Good versus evil. End of story. Growing up the way he had—hand raising animals not strong enough to hack it, and then marching them to their death—he'd learned that every life mattered. He'd seen nature in her raw and unabashed fury, and he knew that only some of the times were clean-cut lines of good and evil. Most often, they were the difference in culture and upbringing. Tyler hadn't chosen this life. It had chosen him. He was good at it, but it took a toll.

When he'd grabbed Khani Slaughter's hand in an unspoken proposition all those months ago, and she'd rebuffed, as she damn well should have, he'd recognized the sick pattern for what it was. He respected the hell out of his lieutenant, but most days, he didn't understand her dry sense of humor or why the hell she wore so much makeup. No way had he wanted her as his own; he only wanted her company as he'd wanted the company of so many before her...to dull the pain of guilt. Guilt, by all accounts, he shouldn't feel.

He stood, replaced the chair, and pulled a sheet of paper from his back pocket.

"What's that?"

"A list of townhouses and condos in decent neighborhoods." He strode to the door.

"Why would you do that?"

"Because surveillance is boring."

"I knew you were watching."

"Sure, you did." He grinned.

Her cheeks flushed, and she ushered him outside with a wave of her hand. He obliged with a nod. "Good day, ma'am."

"Why are you smiling like a fool?"

His boots stalled on the lip of the threshold. "Because you didn't help your argument."

Cara's brow knitted, but she clamped her mouth shut. He waited for a beat and then turned away.

"There are ten years between Rin and me," he tossed back. He walked to the asphalt and then turned. "There are only nine between you and me."

Disheveled hair shook with her denial.

He nodded and smiled.

"That's a lifetime."

"Not from where I'm standing."

"You wanted to know about the cigarettes?"

His head bobbed in confirmation.

"They remind me that nothing we do is without effect. The decisions we make bear out over time. I refuse to make another decision that will hurt the ones I love."

"What if those same decisions hurt you?"

"I don't feel much anymore."

"Your eyes tell a different story." He winked. "I'll see you tomorrow." Before she could protest, he turned and walked away.

Chapter Eleven

A chemical burn worked its way from Cara's nostrils down the back of her throat. At the corners of her eyes, coalescing tears and sweat added to the violent sting, and her lids battled with furious blinks. Black chunks and brown suds covered both her hands. A smudge of dust, dirt, and the ever-present grease lashed the back of her wrist. Specks of tainted water ruined the blouse she'd haphazardly worn to the occasion.

"I thought I knew all of them, but this is a particularly cruel new form of torture." Cara brushed rogue strands of her high ponytail off her cheek with the top of her forearm. She hunched at the waist to bear more weight on the front burner of the food truck's stove and its stubborn halo of baked on fat.

"At least you're upright. The shit keeps dripping in my face." Luck's voice echoed from the oven to her right below the sludge topped griddle.

"Don't let it get in your eyes. You'd go blind. I think I might from the fumes alone." A tear rolled down Cara's nose and dripped onto the stove, creating a tiny clean spot among the swill.

"I thought opening the garage doors would help."

"It didn't." The back double doors hung open, letting in light that streamed from the street but did little in the way of ventilation.

Luck extricated himself from the oven and the narrow alley that ran the length of the truck. He reached around her. Metal screeched against metal, forcing an ache into her molars. He trundled out the back, and seconds later, the food sale window bloomed wide, bringing with it a current of air not exactly fresh but certainly less toxic. The front door to the food truck opened, and Luck stepped inside.

"I thought you'd opened that door already." Cara straightened. After hunched over for so long, the muscles in her lower back protested.

"Never occurred to me." Splatters of brown soiled his face, but it couldn't hide the wide grin that contorted his features, jaw to brows and everything between.

"Are the fumes getting to you? How long were you in here scrubbing before I showed up?"

"Don't get all mom-ish on me. I'm fine, just distracted."

"About?"

"The possibilities." He actually hopped. Not a big leap, but a small fit of excitement his body couldn't contain. His gaze immediately flew to hers. A manly throat clearing followed. "It's open now. Is it better?" Without waiting for an answer, he riffled through a box full of old rags, scrub pads, and various cleaners.

"Yes and no." Dust sticky with layers of oil stuck to the vents above the cook space. Mold grew like grass around the sink's drain.

He looked at her from under his arm.

"For the price, you'd think the truck would've been clean enough to eat off the floor." She pointed at the thicket of dirt covering the stainless steel under Luck's feet. "I'm not eating off that, and I've eaten in some shitholes."

"Oh. No, this isn't that truck." He stood and tossed a rag past her onto the yawning oven door. "I got this puppy for a steal and was able to put back a lot of the money from the sale of the Bentley for inventory and a down payment on a place." His gaze slid over the sink, and his nose crinkled.

Rin and Luck had fought for everything they had. Adversity created character, strengthened dignity. They were proof. Cara didn't want them to fight anymore.

"If you need money, you know—"

"I don't want to touch that money." Luck's staunch tone bounded off the rigid surfaces.

He might as well have slapped her. She wouldn't have been nearly as wounded by that. Pissed? Yes. But not this. The need to vomit toyed with her uvula, but she choked it back.

"*That* money bought the car you sold to buy this truck."

"It's different, and you know it."

Cara knew how he justified his actions. She'd used the same rationale, only to a further extent. Now, things were different. After years of nothing, they were changing fast. Almost too fast for her to keep score. And she ran calculations like a beast. At least, she had until Rin popped back into her life.

"It's just money, Luck."

But suddenly, it wasn't. She knew it. Luck knew it. His unwavering stare said he wasn't backing down until she admitted it.

She tossed the scrub pad onto the counter and turned away. The truck that seemed inescapably small only moments ago stretched. It took too many strides to reach the rear and leap for freedom from the food truck before the sides closed in.

"Cara, I'm not judging you."

Sure.

"I am," she breathed. "Why not you too?"

"That money saved me. It got back your citizenship, your name, and most importantly, Rin."

Cara stopped between the architectural beams just before the exit. Her chest rose and fell too quickly, pulling in noxious fumes.

"It also killed many on my road to redemption"—she shrugged—"or my race for revenge."

"Popov deserved what she got." Luck's voice drew nearer. She wanted to run. Running was her default. His grimy hand wrapped around hers and tugged her away from the street. He turned her to face him and gripped her other hand.

"Gross."

"Yeah." His tongue lolled out in a gag. When he retrieved it, his expression sobered. "I want us to start over. New beginnings."

"You, Rin—you two are young enough for that." She squeezed his hands in return.

"Please." Luck's eyes bulged, and his head levered far back on his shoulders. "If you're young enough to kick my ass—and I shamefully admit you are—then you're young enough for a new beginning."

Cara's head had shaken before he'd finished his pitch. "Not yet."

"When?"

"When I return some money."

Wise investments ballooned her accounts well over the original amount in the last ten years. She'd be fine.

"No."

"No?" Cara glared at him. "You don't want it. Who would, knowing it came from a gang brutal enough to club you in the head for looking at them sideways."

"They'll kill you."

"In case you haven't noticed, I don't die easily."

"They'll use it to further their reach." He dropped her hands and put his on the worn top of his jeans.

"I'm not giving it back to Brödraskapet." Cara's upper lip curled without her consent. "That money belongs to Marina."

"What?" Luck's belly concaved. His shoulders hunched, as though her words had exhausted him. He swallowed a fortifying breath. "Double-crossers deserve a bullet, not a King's ransom."

"You don't know she betrayed us."

More than anything, Cara thought she'd been the forsaker. The young woman's pixie, pale features painted themselves on her brain. Slender frame. Broken blue eyes.

Luck hadn't been Cara's only attempt at atonement. She'd found Marina Sorensen bloody and nearly beaten to death at the end of an alley on an upscale Swedish street corner, a street corner the Brödraskapet had put her on. Motherly instinct had taken over, and before she realized what she was doing, how vulnerable she was making herself and Luck, she'd scooped the girl into a cab and taken her to their temporary home. By the time Luck had returned from a trip where he'd gathered intel on Rin, Cara had bonded with the skittish girl. And none of his objections to the lunacy of taking in a stranger had registered.

There had been no turning back.

To strengthen Marina and acclimate her to their lifestyle, Cara schooled her in the art of survival. Evasion. Tactical. Incursion. Everything.

"You didn't see her face." The gusto of his shout drew Cara from her reverie. Luck wasn't prone to yelling, except when it came to this topic.

"I know things aren't always what they seem," she whispered.

"And sometimes, they are exactly what they seem. You just don't want to admit it."

The clack of heels stilled them both.

"Are you two arguing over my crazy house hunting antics?" Since their house hunting adventure the previous afternoon, Rin had changed her mind about what type of place they should buy at least ten times. Cara's mouth opened to reply, but her daughter giggled. "There's nothing to argue about anymore. Look!" She rushed over to them, waving a piece of paper in her hand. Cara recognized the sheet. "This one has enough space inside *and* out and is in a good neighborhood." She reached them and thrust the page at Luck. "Look."

Rin brushed a kiss onto Cara's cheek. Some of the tension coiled in her belly relaxed. "Thanks for finding this, Mom."

And just like that, the tension returned. "I didn't."

"Who did?" Luck's gaze lifted from the paper and snapped to hers.

"Tyler Grace." No use in hiding it. It didn't matter.

"The Base Branch operative?" Luck's right hand returned to his hip.

"Yes." She nodded.

"You haven't decided to work for them, have you?" Luck's other hand followed suit, holding the

offending sheet between his index and middle
fingers.

"I haven't made any decisions." She gave him
a quick glare. "I'm kind of stuck right now." Rin's
delicate hand warmed her shoulder, drew her
attention, and cooled her temper. She returned
Rin's smile. "In the best spot I've been in, in longer
than I can remember."

"Is he the hot cowboy, the long hair, or the
bulldog?" Rin asked.

Luck snorted.

"I said hot, not melt-my-mind sexy, and
sweet." Rin blew him a kiss and then returned her
attention. "Well?"

Cara stared at her daughter's buoyant smile
and relented. "He's the cowboy."

"Is this cowboy looking for a ride?" Luck
pointed at Cara from head to toe.

Rin gagged.

Shock at Luck's comment quickly turned to,
"Wow. Thanks for the vote of confidence, dearest
daughter."

"She's my mom," Rin said, dividing a shrug
between them. "She's gorgeous and more than
capable of wrangling that if she wanted to, but I
don't need to hear about it."   If Cara didn't have
hands covered in goop, she'd have shielded her face
from the madness. The only people on earth who
knew her—even a little—immediately thought of her
and Tyler Grace as a possible item. They didn't
know her at all. Yeah, she'd been with men younger
than she was, but this was different.

Tyler knew too much about the life she'd led
because, to some extent, he'd led the life too. The
differences between the two placed them on
separate moral strata. Operatives used stealth,
collaboration, and regimented training to complete

their missions. Spies stood before their targets. Callousness, deception, and brutality marked their climb to victory. He'd seen enough to know exactly how she'd operated.

Nope. Tyler Grace was too close to home.

"What I do need to hear," Rin added, "is that both of you are down for house hunting this evening." She plucked the sheet out of Luck's fingers. "I mean all of these are worth a look." Again, her gaze bobbed back and forth between Luck and Cara. He nodded, and Cara smiled. "Great. I'm going to call the realtor." Rin dialed and wandered off as her conversation with the realtor she'd apparently found during the workday evolved.

The moment she was out of earshot, Luck stepped forward. "Do you want me to take care of him?"

"No. I'll take care of him."

Chapter Twelve

She sure as hell would have taken care of him, if he'd shown up as he promised. Only he hadn't. And she wanted to wring his fat neck for it. Tangling with Tyler kept her mind off things more troubling than the easy roll of his hips and how they'd feel thrusting against her skin.

His absence forced her to face too much.

Collateral damage surrounded Cara's life like unflattering lace trim. Her parents had become two large pink bows at her collar. She'd obliterated their lives and left them to rebuild the shattered pieces and care for a bereft child. Her child.

Across the street, the canvas awning threatened to gobble her whole. Its scalloped forest green fringe flapped in the lazy breeze like jagged teeth. A clipart dove spread its wings above the text, Potomac Assisted Living Center. The starched bird gave Cara no peace. Neither did the overcast day nor the calmer temperatures.

Cara had always forced even the smallest thoughts of her parents from her mind. To bear the guilt, to survive, she'd had to force everything but Rin out. If she wanted any hope of a future without the panicky resurgence of crippling shame, there were more people she needed to reconcile with than just her daughter.

The soles of her heels stuck to the concrete, which was farther than she'd made it the last four days. Day one, when Tyler hadn't shown up on her doorstep, and after hours of stewing, she'd allowed herself to think about her deceased mother and dementia riddled father. Day two, when Tyler still hadn't come a-knocking, she'd driven her new rental car to the cemetery where her mother was buried. Buried believing her daughter was dead. Cara had sobbed for the second time in the last week...and the last ten years. She didn't even know the location of her momma's grave. Pathetic.

Day three, she'd driven to the assisted living facility, sat in the car, and logged another pitiful display of weakness before speeding away. That was when she'd caught her new tail. She hadn't tried to lose the full-size SUV. If someone besides Tyler surveilled her, Cara wanted to know who and why. They'd been good, following from so far back that she couldn't discern the make, model, or even the color. When she'd tried to make a block and circle behind them, they'd vanished. This morning, she hadn't seen them, but it didn't mean they weren't there. It just meant they'd changed tactics.

Yesterday, cars had hiked wheels on the curb and wedged into unmarked spaces, trapping others in a greedy jail. Today, Sunday, over half the parking spots were vacant. Still, she'd parked in the auxiliary lot across the street.

Cara shuffled forward until she reached the sidewalk ramp. Would her father remember her? Would it hurt more if he didn't or if he did? Emotion burned her throat. The burden of guilt bogged. Her legs seized.

"Are you going in already? I have to pee."

Every nerve in Cara's body zapped to life. Her head swiveled right to the male rumble that poured

from the open window of a granny-gold Buick
Lacrosse circa 2002. The longhaired Base Branch
operative draped his hefty forearm on the door and
bobbled his brows.

"Nice camouflage." Cara let the sarcasm flow
from her in an ugly wave.

"I thought so." He grinned, unfazed.

She wanted to know why Tyler no longer
watched her, but she refused to ask. It didn't
matter. As much as facing her past hurt, it didn't
create more problems. She'd wanted Tyler out of
her hair since this craziness began a week ago.

"How long have you been following me?"

"A day and a half." Fingers from his other
hand toyed with the dusty blond mustache and
goatee hiding a baby-fresh face. Without all the
hair, the kid would look more like an underwear
model than a certified badass.

Tyler hadn't been on her in four days. She
wondered why there had been a gap in her
coverage. If they suddenly trusted her not to run,
they wouldn't have put Oliver on her.

"Where's Tyler?" What the fuck. She and her
subconscious were going to have a come-to-Jesus
meeting after this. Tyler Grace wasn't her concern.

"You don't need to stall. Your dad will be
happy to see you."

Cara recoiled and her hands balled. The
sudden tension in her back might snap her spine.
She drew a deep breath and studied the operative's
face. He used just the perfect topic to distract her
from the question she'd asked. Goose bumps
traveled up her arm. He didn't want her to know
where Tyler was.

"If his location is none of my business, just
say so. Don't be an asshole."

"It wasn't my intention." He brushed a hand down his facial hair. "I just... A dad would want to know his child's still alive, no matter."

"Do you have children, Oliver?"

"No."

"Then how do you—"

"But I have parents. Parents forgive everything. Their love overrides everything."

Somebody had a rosy childhood. "Not that it's any of your business, but my father may not remember me to forgive anything."

"Alzheimer's?"

"The very devil."

"Go in. You both deserve to find out."

"And you deserve to go to the bathroom?" She glared.

"Yes."

"One condition."

"I don't negotiate."

Cara knotted her arms over her chest. "I can make your job relatively easy."

"Or?"

"Or not." She gave her best disapproving mother expression. The perfect mixture of anger and cold disinterest. Her shoulders bobbed. "Choose wisely."

"Damnit." His fist smacked against his thigh. "I knew I should've taken the UN Summit's security detail." He gripped the steering wheel with both hands. "We don't know."

Her stomach sank. "You don't know what?"

"Where Tyler is." His gaze swung to hers and then bugged. Both hands waved her down as if she was a spooked animal. "He's fine. Don't worry."

Had he seen the five different directions in which her brain had scattered? Nate Harlow, the tiny prick dick, took Tyler as retribution. His extra-large truck slid off the curve, down an embankment, and careened into a lake. One of her enemies had located her and removed her surveillance so they could get a clean shot of her temple. A horse had kicked Tyler in the head, and he lay lifeless in the dirt at that out of the way slice of heaven. Or maybe, just the one. Let him be okay.

"How do you know?" The plea in her voice said she was in over her head where this man was concerned.

"He sent a message a day and a half ago. Once he was good and gone. So no one could stop him."

"What if someone hacked into—"

Oliver nixed the sentiment with a shake of his hairy jaw.

"Nothing's impossible."

"After our last internal breach, yeah, it is. Our fail-safes have fail-safes and firewalls have firewalls." He sighed.

"What if someone forced him—"

"You met Tyler, right?"

"Of course, but no one's infallible."

"Tyler is."

The guy's nonchalance about Tyler's absence crawled up her ass. "What did the message say?"

"Going off grid. Following a lead." Oliver cleared his throat. "Tell Cara, 'Try not to worry about me too much.'"

"Jerk," she whispered. "Big country boy or not, he shouldn't have gone off by—"

"Cara?" She'd recognize the cigar-worn voice anywhere. It had grown shaky and weak, but it still drew her attention as though she were a little girl.

The man sat in a wheelchair hunched forward as if he might tumble right out at the barest bump in the walkway. His unruly salt and pepper pouf had turned into a puffy white cloud. Tears slipped down his droopy eyes, catching between the wrinkles of his nearly translucent skin.

Her sob caught between her fingers.

Behind her, the car started with a quiet grumble, backed out of the space, and rolled away.

A woman bent close to Cara's father's ear. Cotton Lee's head bobbed in slow, jerky movements. When she finally pushed him toward her, in the direction he pointed, he lolled farther to the left, as though the effort had drained him.

The lady in pink scrubs waved a fleshy arm. "Miss? I'm sorry to bother you. So, so sorry, but my patient... Well, this is Senator Cotton Lee." She pointed at her father, as if she wouldn't recognize him.

"I know." Cara stumbled forward under the shadow of the hungry awning.

"Well, I'm sorry. He was sitting by the window and saw you. And you, well, look like... He has dementia and thought you were—"

Cara shouldn't let this woman know who she was, but there was no stopping the crash. Emotional and literal. Her knees buckled. She didn't feel them smack into the concrete, but the echo of impact rang in her ears. "Dad."

"Oh, my God." The nurse clutched her full bosom.

"Jeanine owes me five bucks." His smile was an empty black gap where teeth used to be. It lifted her heart out of her toes and situated it firmly, warmly inside her chest.

"I'll give you a hundred," the woman guffawed.

The wheelchair stopped an inch away. Her dad's shriveled hands lifted to her face, wrapped around her hands, and pulled them from her cheeks. "My Cara."

She hadn't realized she'd hidden her face. "Hi, Daddy." Cara couldn't tell whose hands quivered, but the connection between them shook with a maelstrom of emotions.

"I'll just give you two some time." The nurse pressed the wheel locks into place and patted her father's shoulder. "Senator, you holler if you need me. I'll be just inside." She cast a pointed look at Cara.

Message received loud and clear. Way to wait until it was almost too late. Have you no compassion for the old man? What a shitty daughter.

She was. Cara buried her face in her father's lap. So much of the vibrant, powerful man she'd known had vanished. His career. His teeth. His height. His youth.

"Cara," he cooed. "Don't cry."

Too late. Tears soaked through the blanket covering his legs.

"I'm so sorry, Daddy." Convulsive heaves robbed her of breath. They stung her lungs and scratched her throat. She didn't apologize often, but when she did, it came from the bottom of her soul and ripped a segment of herself free with it.

He stroked her hair and clutched her shoulder. "We don't have much time, Cara."

Instinct overrode sorrow. Cara jerked straight, and her head swiveled. No one approached. At the other end of the facility, an old lady sat on a bench in her Sunday best with a metal walker in front of her. Too many cars in the parking lot had tinted windows. Anyone could be lurking. She reached for the gun at the small of her back.

"Oh, Cara, not because of your enemies. Because of mine."

"What?" Her gaze snapped back to her father. He tapped the front of his head.

"Since Rin came to me with questions about you and concerns about the CIA, I've had longer stints of awareness. I guess hope and fear pumped this old body with adrenaline. But my wits don't stick around as long as I'd like." His cold fingers brushed her cheek. "I knew you'd come back."

"You did?"

"I always thought your working abroad was fishy. After you had come back with a baby yet no pictures or stories to share from your time in Italy, my suspicions grew. When Rin's father came for her, after you protected her" —his kind way of saying killed— "I knew a man in the business and had him do some digging."

A cold sweat broke out over Cara's upper lip. "He shouldn't have told you anything. Nothing."

"Humanity and secrecy are not kin. Never have been. Never will be."

That simple statement held so much truth; Cara gripped the wheelchair to keep from fleeing.

"I knew you wouldn't kill yourself. I knew you wouldn't leave Rin unless it was necessary for her safety."

Fresh air filled Cara's lungs. It soothed the knots in her abdomen from always gasping shallow breaths, as though she didn't deserve the oxygen. Knowing he'd known all those years, that he'd trusted her to do what was necessary to save her child, didn't negate her guilt. It made it easier to bear.

She stared into his hazy, Irish green eyes. He'd given her so much. His unconditional love. His sense of justice. Not quite the value and equality of human life, but no one was perfect. He'd given her daughter stability and the freedom to make her own mistakes. Her father hadn't done it alone.

"And Mom?"

"She wasn't Irish." His head shook, and a hint of a smile curved his sunken lips.

"What does that mean?"

"Your mother, God rest her soul, wasn't as hearty as me or you. I told her you weren't dead. Maybe she knew it all along too." His skeletal shoulders bobbed. "It was easier for her to mourn your loss than to hope for your return."

Tears dripped off the end of her chin. She'd hurt the people she loved so damn much.

"Oh, girl, don't cry." Arthritic, swollen knuckles brushed her cheek.

Cara clung to his hand and pressed it against her chin, desperate for comfort.

"Now. Now. Don't cry. There is so much to be happy about." He turned her chin toward his smiling face, and then shifted it toward the neatly manicured yard and pouring sunshine. "Isn't that right?"

"Yes." A smile stole her sorrow. Her father held no grudge. She hadn't been too late for him. And she'd been given the opportunity to stay and help her daughter build the future she deserved. All she had to do was claim it. Senator Cotton Lee was right again. "So much to be happy about."

"Wonderful." He patted her back, and then straightened in his wheelchair in that crooked manner that was now his norm.

Stiff from kneeling on concrete so long, Cara shifted to stand. Her dad's hand wrapped around her forearm with surprising muster.

"Promise me something, won't you?"

"If I can."

"A spry girl like you shouldn't have any problem placing flowers on my wife and daughter's graves."

The realization that her father was no longer in full command of his mind knocked the wind from her lungs. She collapsed onto her heels. Only his grip kept her upright.

"My secretary will give you the flowers. I bought them on my way into the office this morning and planned to do it myself, but the gaps in my schedule filled to the brim. The people count on me, you know." He slapped her forearm playfully. "It's no trouble finding them just under the skinny oak in the southeast corner of the cemetery." His gaze lifted to the sky. "I lay them together. It's what Miriam wanted. Even though I told her Cara wasn't dead. My little girl will show up one day. I know it."

"And how will you feel when she does?" Cara croaked.

His green eyes focused on her face and then narrowed. He grinned. "Blessed beyond all measure."

Blessed. It should be enough. The time she'd had with him was more than she'd earned. Still, she yearned for more. One more minute to tell him how much she loved him.

"Dear girl, don't be sad. It's a beautiful day. You should take a walk. I wonder if I couldn't impose upon you to stop by the cemetery. My wife deserves some fresh flowers. My daughter too."

It was as if he'd been body snatched by a malfunctioning record player. It was too much. Cara tried to stand but stumbled backward. Her palms met the unforgiving concrete.

The double glass doors flew wide. Her father's nurse ran down the walkway. Both flaps of

Jeanine's scrub jacket flapped in the wind. An avenging angel. "Senator?"

"Yes?" Her father's chest puffed.

Maybe not so body snatched but certainly jumbled.

"It's about that time, sir." Jeanine didn't spare Cara a hiked brow while she whipped back the brakes on the wheelchair.

"Right. The council awaits." He offered his long-lost daughter a small nod. "Good day, miss... Say, forgive my manners. I didn't catch your name."

Cara picked herself off the ground. She ignored her stinging palms and aching knees, and looked into her father's Irish eyes. "I love you, Dad."

His deflated lips parted on a gasp. Cara's lungs stalled, waiting for the flood of recognition.

He licked the bottom of his dry mouth then his gaze slipped away. After reaching left and right, he found Jeanine. "I wonder if I can trouble you for a cup of water?"

"Yes, Senator."

Jeanine pivoted the wheels toward the entrance and set off. Dirt clung to the centerline of the rubber tires. The nurse's white tennis shoes slanted to one side, where uneven steps had rubbed away the outside tread. She pressed a button next to the door, and the door on the right slowly jerked open. When the thing stood wide, Jeanine lifted her crooked shoe to step but faltered. She set it back on the ground and then looked over her shoulder.

"Come back tomorrow. It'll be good for him."

The nurse rolled the chair through the door and down the seeming infinite hallway. It would be good for her father. Jeanine didn't acknowledge it would be hell on Cara. The woman didn't care about that, which was fine. Cara earned the

woman's scorn, and for all her shortcomings, the
nurse cared well for her father. The door closed
with a whack.

Cara would be back tomorrow.

She turned away from the Onyx-tinted
entrance and searched the parking lot for...for the
man she knew wouldn't be there. She shouldn't
want him to be, but she did. So where the fuck was
he?

Chapter Thirteen

Coffee had been a shit idea. Tyler drummed a harried beat on his steering wheel and counted the seconds it took the light to turn green and the line of traffic to get their asses in gear. His nerves rattled more than they had when cornered weeks ago by a group of would-be ninjas in the back alley of a disreputable restaurant in Paju.

It had taken too long. The trip. The light. All of it.

He blinked through the blinding rays of the rising sun. One of the cars slowed, as though feeling their way around the street. Tyler knew exactly where he was going, and these asshats blocked him from the entrance twenty feet away. With a roar, he jumped the curb into the motel parking lot. It jarred him from the seat and yanked the belt across his lap. The reflection he caught in the rearview was a scraggly, sleep deprived madman. Yep, that about summed him up.

Done with stealth, he pulled into the space directly in front of her room, tossed the truck into park, killed the engine, and bailed. Not seeing her for two weeks left him as fucked up on the inside as he looked.

His knock rattled the window on her room and the one next door. Shit. He didn't even know if she was still here. Regulations mandated that he check in, debrief, and get his ass chewed for going off the reservation. Had he done that, he'd know whether she'd stuck close or given in to instinct and run. He'd also be a day or more behind, and he couldn't take one more second without seeing for himself that she was okay. He rapped again, harder.

Slowly, the door opened. The beautiful silver barrel of her CZ greeted him. Odd, but the sight of a gun pointed directly at his heart calmed the bubbling of his gut. The white sheet wrapped around her torso did something else entirely.

Cara's bright sky-blue eyes surveilled him boots to belt buckle, continued to rove over his chest, and finally reached his face. Her peach lips parted on a gasp. "What happened to you?"

"Shoot me if you're going to."

He waited a half beat before shoving the door wide. One step planted his boot between her bare feet. The heat of her thighs burned through the cotton sheet and his well-worn blue jeans. Instead of shooting, Cara lowered the gun to her side and lifted her chin.

Tyler needed no more invitation. His arms wrapped around her back. One hand buried in her tangled locks, the other clamped her tiny waist, and both yanked hard. He pulled her against his front and held her close. The soft mounds of her breasts mashed against his chest, peeking from behind the sheet. The curving crests and a plunging valley ratcheted his frenzy to have her.

Their mouths hovered a breath away. Tyler gave her one last chance to protest, without knowing what he'd do if she did. Combust and disintegrate into a pile of ash. Her fevered breathing buffeted him. The opposite of a deterrent. She was as into this, as desperate for it, as he was.

The time for seduction had passed. Maybe it
had the first time they'd met. Cara wasn't the wine
and dinner kind of girl. He didn't know exactly what
type she was, but he wanted to find out what made
her tick, got under her skin, made her relent
control and succumb to the luxury of her own
satisfaction.

"It's your last chance to shoot," he warned.

"I should. I'd save myself a world of trouble."
Her right hand curled up a fistful of his collar,
drawing them within sparking distance.

"Well?" he growled.

"I've never taken the easy road."

"No use in starting now." Tyler crashed into
her as if he'd been running at full speed. He had.
From HELOs, between airplanes, continents, and
states, he'd sprinted to get back to Cara.

Her lips met his with equal fervor, molding to
his, opening for him, tugging greedily on his tongue
as it forayed into the intoxicating flavor of Cara.

Tyler shoved through the threshold, carrying
her along. He kicked the door closed, and darkness
enveloped them. Losing sight of her severe
cheekbones, striking eyes, and salacious body
sucked.

On the other hand...blindness heightened his
other senses.

Desperation twined with the breaths Cara
panted against his lips. It stiffened her biting grip
on his nape. It pressed the butt of her pistol against
the center of his spine. It rattled between them,
served back and forth from one's frantic heartbeat
to the other.

He locked the bolt and flipped the safety latch
before she pulled him completely under the surface.
It wasn't much security, but it was all he had time
for. Self-preservation drained south with the

roaring of his blood. His rock hard length nestled against her muscled belly and throbbed with every heedless beat.

Tyler stumbled forward like a rookie after a week of basic. The cap of his already sore knee centered against the dresser he'd thought was a few feet deeper inside the room. He recoiled with a grunt. Fuck, he had no idea where he was, except that he was almost exactly where he needed to be.

"I moved the dresser." Cara pressed the words against his lips.

"Why?" Tyler wrestled the sheet up her legs. When he got to their melded hips, the tugging became futile.

"Precaution." Her mouth left his, and she arched away. The bite of metal pressing into his back vanished. A thunk resounded on the hollow wood furniture. Her fingers dug into his waistband, removed his sidearm, and tossed it next to hers with an unceremonious clunk.

"Is someone following you?"

Tyler's hand slid down, grabbed a handful of her tight, covered ass, and lifted. His other hand jerked the sheet from between their hips and bunched it at her waist.

"You haven't been." Cara's fingers clamped onto the tops of his shoulders.

Had she been afraid? Confused? He should have told her where he was going. But she would have bolted. No question.

"I know." The growl rumbled from deep inside Tyler's chest. He pivoted and drove her back against the wall. His lips grazed the edge of her chin before finding her mouth. The hard, thin line succumbed to his unrelenting pressure, turning to soft silk and surprising the hell out of him.

With another urgent yank, the sheet lifted over Cara's butt. His fingers splayed across the hot, smooth skin. Getting warmer.

The heavy globes shook under the force of his hands. He pressed them together, imprisoned them for a pile of seconds, and then skimmed his fingertips along the slick flesh swollen between them.

A telling moue unfurled from Cara's lips. Her hips struggled in the trap of his hold, his body, and the wall. Their lips and tongues battled. Hands crawled down the back of his shirt, collecting handfuls as they went, exposing his heated skin to the tepid air. She pulled it to the back of his neck and used the ends as leverage to roll her hips. That sweet skin glided back and forth over his fingers. Tyler spread her wide, robbing her of the control she had fought so hard to maintain.

This wasn't about control. It was about abandon. He needed her with him, right where he was, totally lost in the bedlam.

Tyler smacked the flat of his fingers across her pulsating clit and full lips with just enough sting to demand her attention but not enough to get him killed.

Cara bucked. Their lips severed the electric contact. Her spine arched, shoving her breasts against his chest. Air clogged in her throat. God, he'd kill to see her eyes. The dilated pools of her pupils. The azure sparks of indignation and savage lust.

She held perfectly still for ten long seconds. Every cell in Tyler's body screamed for release, demanding that he move. He locked down the desire and waited.

The reverse noose around his neck loosened. Cara's hands slipped from the fabric and smoothed over his traps, relinquishing control, giving over to abandon.

So what'd he do? Lost his mind and went straight for his belt buckle. He'd wanted to play her, show her how he could draw it out, how good he could make it for her.

Well, shit.

His pants and boxers hit his boots in a heap, and his dick filled his hand. Thank fuck, he had the presence of mind to rub the crown of his penis over her sex, front to back. The slickness of his pre-cum allowed him to glide easily, teasing her distended nub. Too bad the sleekness of her lower lips opened for him, teasing him right back.

On any other day, he might have tricked himself into believing he'd push inside just a little and then retreat. Today, he gripped her ass, vised her nape, and plunged deep.

Tyler rooted to the pelvis and stilled.

If she cried out, he couldn't hear it over his own groan, the clamor of his own heartbeat, and the wrack of his shattered nerves. She fit him so perfectly. Too perfectly.

Cara's arms looped around the back of his neck, hugging him as tightly to her as she held him inside her. The whoosh of her breaths dueled with the blood coursing through his veins for top billing. Knowing she was with him ripped the little restraint he clung to from his grasp.

"Fuck, Cara."

She whimpered, and that was it.

He retreated the barest of inches and thrust home. The hot satin of her body squeezed him tightly. She restrained him and freed him all at the same time. It was too much.

Tyler backed her against the wall. With his hold on her sweet cheek and neck, he pulled her

close. His face dove into the crook of her neck.
Each deep wave he heaved upon her brought with it
the musk of her sex combined with his sweat. It
shot up his nostrils like a drug, spurring his
excitement.

All sense of decency fled, taken over by
primal instinct. The tempo of his attack rose.
Breaths hitched in Cara's chest. Every impetus
jarred a squeaky moan loose.

"Say my name." The words sounded like
they'd come from someone else. An animal. A man
on the verge of devolving into an animal.

"Tyler."

Bless her. She held him close and called his
name with the carnal intent that matched his own.

The pressure she'd built within him weighted
his balls and then shot up his hammering cock. His
skin stretched. His muscles bulged. He filled her
with his hot cum, without fear of the consequences.
It was a shitty thing to do, to claim her that way
and possibly impregnate her. He knew it. The funny
thing was he didn't care. The only thing he cared
about right now was exploring her, seeing her
come, and then claiming her again.

Using his grip on her nape, Tyler dragged her
mouth to his and let her kiss work its magic. Easy
rolls of her hips helped too. Each movement rebuilt
his need as though it had never been sated.

He walked them toward the bed on quivering
legs. When his shins met the mattress, he released
Cara's cheek. Her legs cinched around his hips,
drawing him into the limits of her body. A syrupy
moan poured from her lips. His fingers fumbled
with the lamp switch. Finally, it clicked and
brought with it a bright pool of light.

Starved for the sight of her, Tyler didn't dare
blink.

Cara's mouth broke contact. Kiss roughened
lips formed a bow, and she levered back. His
constraining hand at the back of her neck turned to
a cradle. He stretched the craving to have her near,
along with his arm, giving her the space she
needed.

The usual sharp blue eyes hazed with lust
morphed in that instant. They widened. Her
haughty brows lowered, dropping the shield she
always hid behind along with them. Her gaze roved
his face and then dropped to their coupled bodies.
The skin at the hollow of her neck bumped with the
winding of her pulse. It beat against his thumb on
the column of her neck.

Tyler moved surely. His free hand untucked
the sheet from between her breasts, dragging the
ear of material across her clavicle. He unwound the
fabric one loop at a time. It unveiled her porcelain
inch by milky inch. Dusky pink areolas called to
that primitive side of him. He relished the
thickening of his dick without giving over to the
urge to move. The sheet landed in a heap on the
floor.

His gaze didn't stop studying every intricacy
of her body. Sharp curves, slow rises. Her wet mons
fisted his length. "Mmm." The stubble burn across
her chin stroked him. Still, he waited for a sign.

As if it had only taken that little sound of
reassurance, like this goddess of a woman needed
reassurance, Cara arched, making the temptation
too much to endure.

Tyler lowered a knee to the mattress. It
groaned under their combined weight as he walked
them to the center. He laid her back onto the bed
and came down atop her, preventing his big ass
from crushing her with a propped elbow.

Though he hated even the thought of leaving her warmth, he couldn't properly explore her lodged as he was. He actually hissed as he withdrew. What a pussy. The corners of her mouth twitched, calling him out.

He grabbed her waist and pulled her forward. Eyes intent on hers, he lowered his mouth to her nipple. That vulnerable mouth opened on a gasp of anticipation.

When she whined, he sealed his lips over her pillowy areola and sucked. Her lids grew heavy, lolling with each tug. His tongue lashed across her small, tight peak. Long lashes fluttered to her cheek. He released her with a loud pop of his mouth, and her lids snapped wide.

"Eyes open, Cara."

Her chin, stained with his loving, jutted. Ever in charge.

His hands found two heaps of her ass and shoved her up the bed. He shoved her legs wide. The heat of his breath coasted over the swollen folds of her vagina but nothing more. He licked his lips, stared at her hot pussy, and then lifted his gaze to her face.

"To think I called you a gentleman." Cara's eyes narrowed, but her belly danced more. The longer he imprisoned her hips and bathed her pretty flesh in his glare, the more it jostled with her panted breaths.

"Uh, eyes on you," she growled the agreement.

"No," he cooed. Tyler dragged the tip of his tongue on either side of her throbbing clit, savoring the taste. He was truly unwilling to deny either of them, even if she didn't relent. "Not if you won't enjoy seeing what I'm doing to you. What I've needed to do to you for so long."

When her hand reached out, he expected her
to grab a hank of his hair and shove his face
against her cleft. Her middle finger grazed delicately
across the gash on his cheek and then the small
cut on his brow.

"Eyes on you," she whispered.

"Eyes open, on us." Something changed in
the tempo of their coupling. The urgency hadn't
vanished, but the intent shifted from salacious to
something more.

With her fierce blue gaze on him, Tyler kissed
Cara's core. Using his lips and tongue, he delved
through her sleek, rich textures. His hands skated
up her hips, finding those tiny nubs. A swift pinch
and tug curved her spine, thrusting her clit across
his taste buds. His hips rocked without permission,
desperate to have her again. But not yet. Back and
forth, her pebbles brushed across his calloused
palms. He molded her small breasts in his grip and
continued to torment her reddened beads, while
laving her clit.

Her head shook slowly and then more
forcefully. Tears pooled at the edges of her eyes.
Every breath strained through a moan.

Tyler retracted one hand from her breasts;
scraping it over her chest, down her abdomen, and
across her mons, he shoved three fingers into her
slick channel to the last knuckle. He hooked them
inside and called her to him with quick, repeated
retractions.

Cara's hips rocked. Her breaths shallowed.
The skin across her chest flushed to an exquisite
hue of pink. Her lips parted around a cry that
shook something loose inside him.

He crawled up her body, thrust himself deep,
and surrendered. They fucked with an abandon
that scared the hell out of him. His arms wrapped

around her waist. His mouth fixed to hers. They rode each other to the brink. Sweat slicked. Saliva pooled. And together, they crashed headlong.

She pulsed around him. Her fingernails dug into his shoulders. Her heels ground against his tailbone. For the second time, Tyler lost himself inside her. He shot off the cliff and leaped into the freefall.

Pulses of cum were still shooting inside Cara when she grabbed his head between her hands and demanded, "What's going on? Where have you been?"

"Jesus." Tyler's forehead collapsed onto her breast. Thank goodness, she didn't fight him on it. One hand released his face while the other cupped his cheek and held him to her bosom. His arm tightened around her until they shook—not from exertion, but from the terrifying realization that he was exactly where he needed to be.

"Well?" Cara had given him half of a minute and probably thought herself quite charitable.

"You're killing me, woman." He brushed a kiss over the soft mound of her breast and shifted his gaze to hers. "Chasing down chatter."

"About?"

Tyler pulled out, retrieved his shirt from the edge of the bed, and cleaned them up as best he could. He'd like to take her to the shower, get her all clean, and then... Cara grabbed his wrist, pulled him back to her chest, and stared him down with a sharply hiked brow. He pressed a kiss to his thumb and rubbed it over her lips.

"You."

Her heart kicked against her chest, reverberating loudly inside his eardrum. "Who was it?" The steel in her voice had returned, but her heart couldn't lie. She was scared, and he hated it.

"North Korea," he said in answer.

"You didn't go inside, did you?" A trill of fear escaped.

"Mmmhmm." He prodded her entrance with the head of his cock and winked.

"Be serious."

"Sorry. Kind of." He nuzzled the valley between her breasts. "I'm crazy, not suicidal. And I'm here, aren't I?" Again, he prodded her.

She purred, momentarily sidetracked. His lips trailed kisses over her neck and up to her mouth.

"I chased it around the border. Spent some time in Paju."

"Ugh."

The way she gagged told him she'd been there on business, not pleasure.

"Popov's captors from back in the day had heard she'd been reported missing and started asking questions."

"So you make sure the answers didn't involve my name."

"No one in the CIA knew she was after you except Nate."

Cara pushed up onto her elbows. He relented and sat, letting her up. Her tongue sucked over her top teeth. "I should have killed him when I had the chance."

"I don't think we needed to. According to the CIA, her target was a Russian defector who was seeking asylum in the States. Consequently, the woman doesn't exist."

"How do you know?"

"I have a friend in London with friends in Moscow. We took a vacation and got some answers."

"I see you did." Her finger tickled his ribs, circling a smattering of bruises. When Cara withdrew her hand, she scooted to the headboard. The longer she looked away, the more she withdrew.

"Hey." Tyler kicked off his boots and pants, crawled to the headboard, and reached for her hand. "I ride bulls. It'll take a hell of a lot more than a handful of thugs to end me."

Cara's pulled her knees to her chest but let him grab her hand. He intertwined their fingers, turning them every which way. They had strong hands. Quick hands. The hands of killers.

"Did you kill Popov?" He didn't really know why he asked since he already knew the answer.

"Yes." She looked down at their joined hands and said no more.

"Just yes?"

"Not just yes." Her pointy gaze sliced him open. "I sleep better knowing that crazy bitch isn't looking for my daughter or me every minute of every day. I tried diplomacy, but it didn't work."

"A North Korean torture camp isn't diplomatic."

Cara retrieved her hand and straightened.

"Popov didn't think so either. And as much as I'd love to take credit for putting her there, her own stubborn vendetta against me led her there. I was in New Guinea." She shrugged and pursed her lips. No sweat off her back.

"Did you leave any trace in North Korea?" He was pushing, but he needed to understand her.

Cara tossed her legs over the edge of the bed and stood. "I didn't make her follow them." She folded her arms over her pretty breasts. "If you have a problem with it—"

"I'm just trying to understand—"

"What?" she shrieked.

Damn. This was exactly how he didn't want this to go. She stood there, indignant and waiting.

"How you, how people can kill without remorse."

"I knew this was a mistake. You need to go."

Tyler opened his mouth to speak, but she stalked into the bathroom and closed the door behind her. A moment later, the shower roared to life.

"Way to go, jackass." He jerked the boxers and pants from the floor and stuffed his legs into them. Next, he stomped into his boots and eyed his shirt. Shirtless Friday, it was.

He fastened his belt, stuffed his gun into his waistband, and headed for the bathroom. She hadn't bothered to lock it. When he yanked back the curtain, the piles of suds on her head, squinted eyes, and wide mouth said she hadn't expected him to hang around.

Cara ducked her head into the spray. Bubbles cascaded down her blond hair and smooth skin. Tyler paid close attention to the sweet dimples above her butt and then the hard swell of her cheeks. His palms itched to get them in his grasp again. Too soon she turned, all trace of surprise gone.

"Luck and Rin are signing on a house this morning. They'll be here in less than an hour."

"I'll drop you off."

"No, you won't."

He canted his head, studied her for a minute, and then nodded.

"What does that...look mean?" She rubbed a hint of soap from her lips.

"I'll give you space. I'd leave you alone if you really wanted me to."

"I want you to leave me alone."

A fat smile stretched his sore mouth.

"What now?"

"At least, your kiss doesn't lie." He blew her one, closed the curtain, and left her to her own devices. For now.

Chapter Fourteen

Why did he have to be right, damnit?

Cara banded her hair into a high ponytail and tried her best to ignore her reflection. The stray wisps she smoothed back didn't count. Her knowing gaze did, though. So did the luggage bags hitching a ride under her eyes. Sleep hadn't come easily for the last two weeks. Last night, it hadn't come at all. Her gaze caught on the freshly made bed. Instead of wasting a night wallowing in their combined scents on the sheets, she should've retrieved the linens after returning from the day spent in a real estate lawyer's office and then cleaning their new house.

His scent was gone, but the feel of his hand on her skin, of him filling her, would haunt her for the rest of the day. Along with the question—how could he lose himself with her while thinking her heartless?

The hairbrush landed with a clatter on the vanity counter. She wanted nothing more than to pick it up again and slam it onto the counter repeatedly. Once upon a time, she'd orchestrated the fall of a government. These days, she couldn't govern her own emotions.

My, how the mighty had fallen.

Her phone beeped, alerting her to another text message. The knot of nerves behind Cara's eye sockets loosened. Rin had been texting for the last hour, asking her opinion on everything from paint colors to mothballs. Eight out of ten questions, Cara googled before responding. No way was she a Holly-Homemaker expert, but to be included, needed... It was everything. She didn't need anything more than her children.

Cara abandoned the frazzled woman in the mirror, collected her pouch purse, and slung it across her chest. Worn khaki shorts, an equally threadbare T-shirt, and sneakers didn't allow much room for a concealed weapon. She refused to ruin another outfit that concealed while helping her kids move into their new house.

Head down, she read Rin's message while she headed for the door. 'Luck says pile it all into the food truck and make one trip. It still smells like bleach. I say we pack each of our cars and make several trips. You're the deciding vote.'

She opened the door and chuckled. "Way to shove me in the middle."

"Well, darlin', if you sit in the middle, that'll give us more room for their stuff. It'll also give me a chance to cop a feel."

A wave of gooseflesh coursed over her skin, and her head snapped up. Tyler Grace screamed moonshine and line dancing as he leaned against the passenger side of his truck, a gooseneck horse trailer jointed into its bed. One booted heel propped on the back tire, he had the tip of his opposite thumb hooked into the loop nearest his massive belt buckle, and his other arm draped over the edge of the truck bed.

Saliva and irritation pooled in Cara's mouth.

"But we'll start with a shotgun. Let you warm up to the idea." His brows waggled as he shoved off

the truck, sauntered to the passenger door, and
opened it.

"I told you I wanted you to stay away."

"Yeah." He nodded. "I heard the lie."

"Why are you here, Tyler?"

"Because I like the feeling I get when I'm near
you."

"A hard-on? Hold that thought." She
unzipped her purse and shoved her hand inside.
"I'll give you a few hundreds. You can take them to
the titty bar and get the same feeling."

"Cara." A warning current pulled on her
name. When she looked up, the hood of his brow
had darkened his sweet green eyes, and a muscle
ticked in his jaw. "It's more than that, and you
know it."

Her stupid heart bumped.

She stepped back and stumbled over the
sidewalk.

"You're not a coward, and you no longer have
valid reasons to vanish. Don't run." A hint of
desperation peppered his timbre, and it sparked
her rage. Her spine stiffened.

"Why not? Why are you being nice to me,
giving me gifts, and doing things for me?" She
pointed at the trailer he intended to use to move
her daughter's things. "Why are you fucking with
my head?" Cara's hand should have landed on her
forehead, but damn it all, it flew to her heart. "Why
bother when I'm a heartless killer?"

He stepped forward and grabbed her hand
before she could gather herself enough to retreat.
His fingers interlaced hers, while his other hand
grabbed the back of her neck and held tight. That
green gaze lowered to hers.

"I don't think you are heartless, Cara. I
wanted to know how you separate the two parts of

yourself." His lids lowered and squeezed for a long second before opening. "I can't separate it, and it's killing me."

Her heart picked that moment to plop into a sopping heap onto the ground. She could blame it on the lack of sleep and pheromones, but the bone-deep ache in her chest told her it was so much more. This courageous man revealed his innermost demons, and she'd give up her life to slay them.

Fuck.

"Tyler, this work isn't for everyone."

"I know." The square of his jaw waggled. "I'm good at it, and I do good things too."

"It's the only thing that's kept you above water this long."

His grip on her neck slipped into her hair. He nodded and pulled her closer.

Cara let herself go. She removed the hand from her heart and placed it over his. "You know, this smartass asked me once, what if those same decisions hurt you? Same goes. What if the good you do hurts you?"

"I don't know."

Tyler tipped up her jaw with his thumb and drew her near.

The phone sandwiched between her other hand and his belly beeped. She jumped, pulled her hand back, and glanced at the screen. Another message from Rin. 'What's your vote?' It beeped again. 'We have fruit, eggs, biscuits, and coffee.' And again. 'Where are you?'

He grazed a kiss over her brow. "Someone's impatient. Let's go." His hand slipped from her hair to the small of her back and ushered her toward the open door. "I wasn't kidding about the middle seat."

"Or copping a feel?" she asked.

"I never kid about that." Tyler hoisted her
into the seat and handed her the belt. "Safety first."
The words practically lodged in his throat before
they'd fully exited. "Well, usually." He closed the
door, rounded the truck, and climbed in on his
side, guilt shortening his movements.

Safety. Sex. He thought he could have gotten
her pregnant. Understanding hit her like a five-ton
truck with a fully loaded trailer at its back. It
wedged her heart in her airway suffocating her of
oxygen and the love she'd dared to entertain for this
man. For this young man with his entire life ahead
of him. With a wife. With children. His own flesh
and blood. And most definitely without her.

Saved from speaking while he maneuvered
the rig through the parking lot and crowded streets,
Cara focused on regulating her heart rate, nausea,
and breathing. After he had eased onto the
interstate, he turned toward her. The edge of his big
bottom lip clamped between his teeth as he was
about to delve into a topic she couldn't bear to
discuss. She let him have it.

"Why aren't you a cattle rancher in
Kalamazoo?"

His lips mashed together for several seconds
before relaxing. "My analytical skills were off the
charts in high school. I was recruited off the stage,
and here we are."

That explained why he'd gotten the jump on
her in the warehouse the first time they'd met. It
also probably meant he knew she was stalling from
the serious conversation, but it didn't stop her from
asking him a hundred different questions by the
time they reached the place it had all started—the
warehouse.

Cara kept her distance the rest of the day by
putting the men in charge of moving the furniture

and big boxes, while the girls focused on unpacking boxes and item placement. By the time it was all said and done, the sun had slipped toward the other half of the world. They all looked bedraggled and felt it too.

For a moment, Cara thought about bidding Tyler good night and staying behind. At least until he'd left and she could catch a cab or get one of the others to take her home. But who the hell was she kidding? She didn't have a home. She had a shabby room in a shoddy motel, a bag of clothes, and not much more to her name. Besides, she needed to get rid of him once and for all. No more leading him or herself on.

She tried to do it on the interstate and then again at a streetlight while he was in the middle of a story about his, Oliver, and Hunter's first mission. Every time, a thick lump formed in her throat.

The truck rumbled into the motel parking lot.

Cara's heart pulsed in her belly.

"Isn't it about time you found your own place," he said.

Simultaneously, she cursed and thanked God. Cara narrowed her gaze and cut him with it. "One roll in the sack and you think you can—"

"Whoa." His hands came up and settled her as if she was a skittish horse. "All I think is you're racking up one hell of a hotel bill that you could use for a down payment or to put away to pay for a wedding venue."

Why did he have to be so sensible and make this so hard? Why couldn't he get pissed at her getting pissed and leave? Because he was analytical and not a hothead.

"If you're not going to take the Bureau's offer, I know people outside the industry. We could find you a job in a minute if money's a problem."

Money and the Bureau hit on sore subjects.
She used the angst from them and the pain of
knowing she couldn't have what she wanted so
desperately.

Cara iced out every emotion but anger.

"Look, Tyler. You're a good lay. You're even
easy to talk to, but if you're not man enough to
blow a madman to bits and sleep better knowing
you've done your part for your country, then you
won't be able to handle me. I kill first. And usually
don't ask many questions. But thanks for
everything and good luck."

She wound the long, thin strap of her purse
around her hand, squeezed as hard as she could to
keep the tears at bay, and opened the passenger
door. Before he could say a word, she'd slipped her
thighs off the leather. Her heart bore the brunt of
the impact with the asphalt. Cara slammed the
door and bolted to her room without looking back.

After fumbling with the key, she let herself in,
closed the door, and double locked it. Her breaths
caught in her windpipe. The short, hiccupping
pants stung almost as much as the tears that
streamed over her cheeks, blurring the dim room.
She slid down the door, covered her face, and cried.

Chapter Fifteen

Each sob fractured Tyler's heart. For all the fucking analytical skills in the world, he'd never understand women. Especially not one as complex as Cara was. He wanted to, though. He sat with his back to hers. A door between them. A door and something else that had nothing to do with his tenderhearted tendency toward taking lives.

When he'd confessed what he'd only ever whispered to himself, her vibrant blue eyes had locked on him with something far from repugnance. He didn't know what the look meant, but nothing could top the way it wrapped around him like a full body embrace.

The shift in her had come after he'd made the comment about safety. Immediately, she'd quieted, and then when made to talk about the subject, she had shifted away from her to him, or the move, or Rin, or Luck, or anything except what truly ate at her. He should have forced her to face him, it, whatever she needed to battle before she could be free. Had he, there wouldn't be an ever-widening gap between them.

But really, before he could expect her to face her demons, shouldn't he face his?

"Growing up on a farm, I learned to nurture life. I bottle fed calves whose mothers died in labor. I spent nights in the barn with sick baby goats.

Sure, some of them didn't make it, and then later, I realized what my family did with the cows after they came of age. I also learned animal CPR and worked on everything from horses to cats. When I was in junior high, I worked illegally in our family veterinarian's clinic, knowing that's what I'd do with my life. Then the perfect storm hit."

He didn't know if she could hear it all or if she'd even care. It didn't matter. "Half our herd came down with Bluetongue. We spent a fortune properly quarantining, making enclosures, subdividing fields, and creating boundaries. And then there was the cost of spraying to eradicate the ugly little bug infecting them. Next, Oprah announced to the world she'd never again eat beef because of the outlandish practices of some factory farms and the cattle market took its biggest hit since the Great Depression. Then the fucking test came along."

Her sobs had stopped.

"Suddenly, my parents were up to their eyeballs in debt, and I had the option to have my education paid for and a job that assured my future. I never realized how much I resented everything about how it went down. I hate killing, but maybe I hate that it wasn't my choice more."

Tyler scrubbed a hand down his face and took a deep breath. "Huh." His head bobbed. A bit of the weight lifted from his chest. "I know what I have to do, Cara. What do you need to do?" When he stood, rocks and dirt scraped under his boots. He looked at the door for a long minute, hoping it would open but knowing it wouldn't.

"Figure it out, darlin'. See you in the morning."

Chapter Sixteen

"Seems we need to do a better job of disorienting people when they have on those black bags." Vail Tucker exited a bleak conference room, all hard, cold surfaces, and strode down the hallway toward her. A striking woman in kickass leather pants, vivid red lips, and a fuck-off scowl departed behind him. Her aggressive pace overtook the Base Branch director in three long strides.

Cara's heart rate kicked. Her breathing evened, and her muscles loosened, ready for anything.

"Bloody time you came to your senses, Lee. Welcome aboard." The woman's barbed British accent took its prick of flesh and blood, while she maintained the stormy stride past Cara down the hall and around the corner.

"Don't mind Khani. She's looking for her brother, after just finding him and losing him again." Tucker skirted the corner and headed toward his office. The flick of his head stood as her formal invite.

"I imagine she'll find him before long. She's determined."

"Among other things," he agreed.

"I also imagine I'm not the first to find their way back after the black bag roundabouts." Cara followed Tucker into his office and closed the door behind her.

"The good ones, the ones we want, always find their way back." He placed a stack of files on his desk. She read each label in a quick glance. US Elite. Anosov Sadovsky. Classified. What an interesting combination, especially the one without a label that was stamped classified. Tucker lowered his head, catching her curious gaze in the act. "Can I get you anything. Coffee? Water? A pillow? It's moved past late to pretty damn early."

"And you're still here." She looked around the sparsely decorated space.

"I am. And I'll catch hell about it from my girls, but cooking them a big breakfast should save my hide."

"Do you usually stay 'round the clock?"

Tucker folded his arms and propped a hip on his desk. "I'm not going to lie. There have been weeks when I haven't seen the light of day. Most of them were because I didn't care to. Now, it's easier to leave. I have something to go home to."

"How long am I going to have a babysitter?" Cara braced her legs apart and folded her own arms. "Until I accept the job? What if I decline?"

"Khani is heading back to London, and we need someone incorruptible with field experience, undercover prowess, and socio-political understanding." A smile tugged at the corner of his mouth.

Basically, yes. She was stuck with Tyler until she agreed or fled. Not much of a choice now was it.

"The last time I was here, you told me to live my life." Cara swallowed the emotion creeping into her voice. "I don't know what that is anymore." Anger shored up the edges.

His arms uncoiled and folded at his waist.

"I'm still figuring it out. Nearly fifteen years
ago, my wife and unborn child died as a result of
the work I did."

"So I'm S.O.L.?"

"No." His salt and pepper head shook. "It
takes time…signing a truce with your past and
looking at the future." He stopped for a minute and
then swallowed. "The truce is a real bitch."

"Pull Grace off me. I'll work for you. I just
need some time to handle something before I start,
and I need distance from this organization to do it."

"Fair enough." Tucker stood and offered his
hand. "Just know, if you need anything, we protect
our own and are at your disposal."

"Thank you." She took it, not at all surprised
by the strength behind the gray hair, proper suit,
and blue tie.

Cara's phone vibrated in her pocket. Nausea
gagged her with every vibration. The only person
who would call her at this hour wouldn't call
because she'd hurt him deeply. Two other people
had her number. If they were calling in the middle
of the night, the news couldn't be good. She
whipped the phone from her jeans and checked the
screen. A blocked number. For a split second, she
thought about not answering, but this was no
telemarketer. This call was deliberate.

"Until our upgrade, our phones didn't work
behind these thick walls. The new system allows us
to funnel the calls, detect any tracking software,
and reroute it."

"Fancy." Cara said the word but didn't hear
anything except the insistent vibrating. She
initiated the call and placed it on her ear. "Hello?"

"I'm sending you an email. You'll especially
enjoy the attachment," an enhanced voice said over

the line. "I've been waiting for you, Cara. Don't make me wait any longer."

Someone found her. When you live in the open and have as many enemies as she'd gained over the years, what else could you expect?

The room chilled twenty degrees, freezing her to the marrow.

Please God, don't let them have found Rin.

If only the cold brought with it an anesthetic. It didn't. Every breath scalded her lungs. The simple act of depressing the screen to disconnect the call hurled a surge of caustic terror through her body. Nerves clattered together, creating chaos out of calamity.

She swallowed fetid saliva. The haunting email sat boldly unopened at the top of her inbox. Something so innocuous held such power over her. She reviled the feeling so much that it lent her strength enough to press the subject, *My Shame.*

Inside, the body blinded with its static white. The two attachments lanced her heart.

Chapter Seventeen

The file attachments next to one another at the bottom of the email showed no thumbnail image. Each had its own label.

Tyler. Marina.

Cara clicked on the first. A small window appeared with an opaque play button. Behind it, Tyler hung in the dark barn. His hands coiled with a rope stretched above his head. A floodlight illuminated his taut expression, the rage in his gaze, his naked body, and the blood coating his skin.

The impact knocked her back, forcing her to plant both feet on the ground and face the devastating reality.

She loved Tyler. And she might never get the chance to love him.

"Everything okay?" Tucker stepped forward.

The action kicked Cara out of her petrified stupor. Her gaze tore away from the grim scene, and it met Tucker's knowing eyes.

Was Marina a victim in all this or the orchestrator? She didn't know. The two possibilities spelled out two very different ends for the girl.

"I have to go make peace with my past...or kill it." She headed for the door. "Call me in ten minutes. I'll know more then. I'm borrowing a car. A fast one. You can have one of your guys bring me the keys, or I'm wiring the thing. Oh, and drop that security wall. I don't have time to screw with it."

"Cara." His voice wasn't loud, but it demanded her attention.

She didn't want to give it. It took time, and she had to hotwire a car and drive a distance that a few weeks ago had taken her and Tyler more than an hour. Her hand landed hard on the knob and jerked the door open, but she spared Tucker a glance.

"I have a chopper headed to base with two agents. If you'll wait, it's yours."

"How far out?"

"Twenty minutes."

"Does it have to refuel?"

"Yes."

She calculated the numbers. If she pushed, she could get there faster. The drive might kill her, but it would be hard and fast. Sitting around would turn life into a torturous series of milliseconds.

"No go," Cara decided.

"Then take this." A key fob sailed through the air in her direction. On instinct, she snagged it before it hit her.

"Thank you."

"Thank me by bringing it back in one piece. Take a right out of the bank of elevators. It's next to the red truck."

If she needed to drive—what was apparently Tucker's personal car—through a battlefield to save the people she loved, she wouldn't hesitate. Instead of making false promises or wasting any more time, Cara sprinted to the staircase. She gripped the rail and leaped. The balls of her feet grazed every third step on her climb up three levels to the parking garage. Reverberations of her labored breaths echoed off the concrete.

The metal door smacked into the wall from the brunt of her exit from the stairwell out onto the lot. Her feet didn't slow. She depressed the unlock button and ran full tilt toward a sleek black Audi parked next to another monstrous truck. What was it with people in this country and their hulking automobiles?

Her thumb held the phone's center button until it beeped. "Call Luck."

"Did you mean call Luck?" the robotic voice asked.

"Yes! Mother fuck."

"What's wrong?" Luck answered after one ring.

"Gear up and meet me at the coordinates I'm texting you right now. And don't bring Rin." She hung up before he could ask questions. She didn't know answers yet anyway, but she needed him moving toward the location.

Cara threw open the driver's door and dove inside.

Once belted in, she put every rumbling horse to the test. The suspension got its workout too. The engine growled, and the tires screeched, but it weaved through traffic like it was in a Nascar race —bumping other cars, boxing them in, and pushing hard toward the finish line. When the wheels hit the highway, her furious grip on the steering wheel loosened enough for her to grab the phone that had skittered onto the floorboard during a particularly stunning maneuver that left a mark on Tucker's car she'd be paying back a long, long time.

Her hands—so sure moments ago playing chicken with her life—quaked. The slender metal phone shook with each command her fingers gave. Finally, the email opened. Cara diverted her gaze from Tyler's video and clicked on the second attachment.

It wasn't a video, but a still shot of Marina bathed in a pool of light. The same kind of rope Tyler had used to truss up Nate bound her hands above her head. A length of the rope coiled twice between her parted lips. Tears soaked the girl's lashes. Mania plagued her eyes.

The sight of Marina in pain twisted Cara's guts. Betrayed or not, she cared about the young woman.

Cara gripped the phone between her thumb and index finger, hooked her other fingers around the leather wheel, and clicked on Tyler's attachment. Too soon and, somehow, too many stilted moments later, the screen burst to life.

A car she dashed past—a little too closely—blared its horn. The driver probably gave her the finger, but she didn't see it. Her gaze locked on the image of Tyler's face, and it ate up the entire display. Lines creased his brow. His full lips stretched thin over blood-coated teeth.   But he didn't make a sound. Not the breaths puffing his cheeks nor the agony pouring from his expression let loose a note.

"He's so tough, Markus." The deep voice, so close to the camera, shook the speakers in her phone. Then the camera panned right.

"No," Cara barked, willing the large man that stepped into the full frame to be anyone but Markus Royan.

The sick son of a bitch didn't kill people. He destroyed them. He stripped them limb from limb until he bared their soul and then crushed it from existence.

Cara had made the unfortunate acquaintance of Markus and his brother, Tor Royan five years ago in Sweden. They'd been Marina's pimps and none too happy with Cara for stealing away their best girl. Never mind that one of their customers had left Marina for dead. They'd have preferred it that way. With her death, they'd have owned the rich bastard for the rest of his miserable life and replaced Marina by day's end.

On Marina's behalf, she'd forced a bargain on the brothers that had left them pissed but, ultimately, hog-tied…as Tyler would put it. Forget Marina or have their every foreign and domestic bank account drained and donated on their behalf to various battered and underserved women's groups across the world.

Tor, in particular, had taken the news hard. He was accustomed to being the deviant, dismantling people's lives with blackmail and manipulation.

As it turned out, he'd gotten the last laugh.

A year to the date of Marina's final liberation from the Brödraskapet backed brothers, she'd turned on them without warning.

Cara had followed through with her promise, siphoning six million dollars off their accounts. She'd distributed it through world organizations that helped women and kept enough to bankroll her own cause, keeping Rin safe. In essence, she'd had the last laugh. The second knife wound in her back made it hard to breathe, much less find the humor in the situation. Duplicity—first, from her country, and then, from the broken girl she'd looked upon as a daughter—ruined her ability to trust once and for all.

And now, she watched the demon loom frightfully dark over her future. Over Tyler. A man she trusted, despite herself.

The camera panned right, away from the man she loved and away from the agony he silently dueled.

Markus's six-foot-five, 320-pound form stepped into the shot. The smile on his split lips ripped the beating heart out of Cara's chest and hoisted it into the air in victory.

"Yeah, real tough." Markus's ominous boom reverberated through the video and then through her bones.

"He's ruining your reputation," a man in the blurry, black background jeered. Several oohs and laughs followed, turning torment into entertainment. Toss in beer and they'd have a party fit of a pub.

How many of them were there? A lot, considering they'd taken Tyler as a hostage. Though not unscathed by the looks of Markus's mangled face.

Cara's molars nearly cracked under the pressure of her impotent rage.

"Fools. You don't understand a thing." Markus turned toward the crowd. He bent at the waist, folding his broad belly in two, and hefted the board she'd strained every muscle to heave off the barn's door latch as if it was a nine iron.

"No." Cara whispered the futile prayer.

"The more he resists, the sweeter his relent will be." He waggled the end of the board, a batter readying for his line drive. The cameraman hustled backward, widening the shot and bringing Tyler back into view. "And when I break him, Cara will have no choice but to come." Markus's ice blue gaze found the camera. "I know how you love fixing the broken."

Muscles and meat stretched the dingy white shirt binding Markus's hammy biceps. He wound the large plank back around his head.

Cara's heart stilled. Her lungs stuttered. The blood in her veins fermented.

Markus backloaded the board. His front biker boot lifted off the ground. The sneer on his gruff face compounded with his effort.

Every taut muscle in Tyler's body formed a topographical map that screamed.

Clamped lips.

Bulged veins.

Angry ridges.

Canyons of furor where the eye used to be.

Markus released the raging force Cara had fueled. The small hunk of tree parted the air like a bolt of lightning. Its impact landed in the middle of Tyler's thigh. The bone under a mountain of thigh muscles split, birthing thunder that rolled through the miles, knocking a roar from Cara's chest.

Tyler's clamped lips turned ashen white. He gulped air.

"What was that?" The cameraman moved in tight. "Do you want to scream? Cry?"

"Cara." Tyler pushed her name through clenched teeth.

"Aww. He wants his girlfriend," the cameraman announced to the group.

"Me too," one of the men said with a lewd tilt to his voice.

"Don't come for me." Tyler had breathed the words before his body went slack.

Cara's eardrums trembled. Her throat ached. She dropped the phone into her lap, unable to watch more. The steering wheel shook under her grip. She heaved a breath and forced it through her larynx again.

A litany of curses filled the car, for herself, for her regrets, but mostly, for Markus Royan. Dead man walking but not for much longer.

The phone rang, shooting another dart of adrenaline through her veins.

"What?" she answered.

"If you don't make it there in one piece, Tyler's chances of rescue decrease. Stop driving like a lunatic. Do you know how many favors I've had to offer to keep your ass out of jail? I'm leveraged up to my eyeballs with the D.C. Metro Police. It'd better be worth it because I won't see straight for—"

"How do you know they have Tyler?" Cara's voice cracked. She couldn't handle another turn of treachery.

"We hacked your phone."

That she could handle.

"How do you know the Royan brothers?" Tucker demanded.

"Marina Sorensen. They have her too."

"Who is she? She's not in our system."

"She's an innocent." The moment the words exited her lips, she knew they were false. At one point, Marina had been innocent, but now, she was as unassumingly deadly as Cara was. So why had she stayed with the brothers, and why had they turned on her?

"That's the barn at the Sanford's house, right?"

"Correct."

"Why there?"

"Nate Harlow."

"I don't understand, but you can explain later. There are at least five of them and two possible hostages. You can't go in alone."

"I'm not. Luck is meeting me."

"I'll pretend I didn't hear that but hear this. I have two of my guys in a HELO hot on your heels. If you need to wait for them, wait. And don't shoot them."

"Tell them not to get in my way and I won't."

"Won't wait or shoot them?" Tucker asked.

"Either."

***

"How the hell did you get here so fast in this thing?" Cara waved Luck into the passenger seat of the white panel van he'd used for surveillance through the years while keeping an eye on Rin.

Luck wore green digital camo with a loaded vest and belt.

"It sprouted wings once or twice, but I just got here." He crawled over a black vest with all the trimmings and into the other seat. "I was twenty miles closer than you were so that helped a lot. That and I had everything packed for the move. I tossed a few cases and boxes in the back."

His hand wrapped around the vest's shoulder strap and then lifted. "This is for you."

"They'll just make me take it off before they let me in." Cara shifted the car into drive and gunned the engine.

"Now, you care to tell me what the hell's going on?"

The driveway came up fast. It tended to happen that way when you drove in aggressive excess of the speed limit. She wheeled the van onto the gravel drive.

Luck braced both hands on the dash.

"Markus Royan is holding Tyler and Marina to get to me."

"Son of a bitch." Luck glared out the window at the horses in the fields. He didn't stare long. As fast as Cara drove, they morphed into blurry specs.

"At least they don't have Rin."

Cara had thought it, but couldn't, wouldn't, say it aloud.

"No disrespect to Tyler."

"Let it go," Cara ordered. "We're here." She slowed at the divergent paths of the driveway in front of the house.

"So what's the plan?"

"Get down." She shoved his head between his shoulders. "Don't get shot and shoot some people."

"Detailed as ever." He sliced a sharp gaze toward her but froze part way.

"What's wrong?" Her foot slipped off the accelerator.

"Rin," he squeaked.

"What? Was she pissed?"

"No."

Which meant her daughter was probably really, really pissed at both of them.

"What are you doing here?"

Luck's words circled Cara's brain once without sticking to anything. They didn't make sense until they did.

Cara slammed on the brakes halfway between the large pergola and the barn and whipped around in her seat. Her daughter grimaced from a knotted ball behind the driver's seat.

"I'm sorry. But I thought you were disappearing again, and I wanted to stop you." Rin looked at Luck and then back to Cara. "He wouldn't tell me what was going on, so—"

"Because I didn't know, but I knew it wasn't safe for you—"

"Oh?" Rin wrenched her torso from the floor. "So it's not safe for me, but it's safe for you?"

"We have training—"

Cara lifted her hand, cutting off Luck's retort and Rin's defense. She pulled her daughter close while making certain she stayed seated on the van floor. Her fingers framed Rin's striking face—a younger, more tenacious version of her own—and the smooth skin cooled Cara's palms.

"Rin, I'm not leaving you ever again, if I can possibly help it. Do you hear me?" Cara coughed to keep the emotion out of her voice.

"Yes," Rin whispered.

"And if I do leave you, know it wasn't at all what I wanted, but it was what I'd give a thousand times over to keep you safe."

Tears rolled down her daughter's cheek in quiet, heavy waves. Rin's fingers tightened around hers, unwilling to let her go.

Cara bent and pressed a kiss to each of her daughter's cheeks.

Then she twisted her hands free from Rin's and scrambled from the van.

"Get her away from here," she told Luck. "If it all goes sideways, Tucker will protect you."

Luck rushed into the driver's seat and nodded. She read sorrow and disappointment, anger and determination on his features. He slammed the door and threw the van into reverse. Gravel kicked up from the tires. A cloud of dust shrouded Cara. The farther Rin moved away from her, the more her heart ached, but peace edged the pain. Her daughter was safe, which was all she'd ever wanted.

If she could save Tyler, it would be more than she deserved.

Cara faced the barn and spread her arms wide.

"Let them go! I'm the one you want."

The shot came from the dark barn doorway. Cara didn't see it coming, but she heard it. She also felt it rip through her chest.

Chapter Eighteen

The bullet weighed a thousand pounds. Her feet shuffled sideways, digging into the gravel to stay upright, but it didn't help. Pressure crushed her chest cavity. Without awaiting orders, her knees buckled. On impact, the rocks ripped holes through her pants and the flesh covering her patellas.

Cara heaved a breath. A wheeze flirted with the air around her but didn't fill the burning need for oxygen. Her crash continued in sluggish succession, pivoting the horizon. It sucked her to the dirt.

A week ago, Cara would have given herself over to fate. Content in the knowledge that she'd given her life for her daughter's, she'd have let gravity drain the blood from her body and welcomed the darkness. But she had more to live for than just her daughter. Dammit, she had herself to live for and the promise of more adventures to come. She was tired of living alone, hiding in shadows.

Cara lifted her left hand and shoved her middle finger through the fabric of her shirt and the skin slicked with blood. She plugged the hole at the top right of her chest. Her face met the edge of the grass. The scent of pollen and blooms filled her lungs. Dewy blades clung to her cheeks and tickled her open mouth.

Several pairs of footsteps approached.

She'd landed facing away from the barn. Not that she was inclined to make a tactical move. With her gun in her waistband and a hole in her chest, she might kill herself trying to reach it.

Hard as it was, Cara calmed her breathing and held perfectly still.

The crusher had tried to end her without a show. Maybe it was the low oxygen level or shock setting in, but she couldn't wrap her head around the fact that he'd used a gun and aimed it close to the heart. After all, Markus used videos like the one he'd sent her of Tyler to propagate his reputation and strike fear into the hearts of those in his employ and business ventures. It was why she hadn't bothered with stealth. She expected to have time before the death blows came.

"That was for my brother," Markus called from across the lawn. "If you survive it, this next part will be for me. Dead or alive, you're just the thing to break the tough guy inside. Harald and Eric, bring her in. But first, check her for weapons. Even if she's passed on."

One of the men heading her way gave a grunt. Another said, "Inga problem," which meant   no problem. Cara hadn't yet decided how she was going to be a problem. Until her heart stopped beating, she would be one.

"Emil," Markus barked, "take the car. Catch the van and kill whoever's inside. Run them off the road, if you can. Make it look like an accident. Unless you can't. If not, get it done and get back here."

Not a chance. If she knew anything about Luck—and after seven years on the run together, she knew him better than she knew her own daughter—he'd get Rin to safety and at the very least set up a defensive position. And if he trusted Rin to stay out of sight, he'd come back with a boom or two. Whether she could hang in there until he got ready was another matter altogether.

She hoped so. For her sake and Tyler's.

The first set of footsteps hit gravel.

Nerve endings in Cara's torso caught fire. Sweat broke out over her skin. A hiss threatened to bleed out between her teeth.

Surprise was the only thing Cara had going for her if shot and breathless on the ground could ever be considered an advantage. Her eyes opened. She stared blankly at the cloudless blue sky.

Several yards away, a car engine rumbled to life.

A shadow cast over Cara's face. It eased the sting of not blinking.

"I'll get her feet," a grumpy grumbling voice harrumphed.

"What's wrong with you?" the second guy asked.

"Roland and Peter are dead, for starters."

"We didn't know who that guy was, only that he was banging Cara."

"Yeah, well, we learned too late for them."

Tyler had given them a run for their money. Good. It gave her strength to wait, and when it was time, she'd make her move.

"That it?"

"Our brothers are dead."

"And," the other man coaxed.

"Emil always gets the good job, and we get stuck with this."

"I knew it was about Emil. It's always about Emil. He has rank. Be sore if you want, but he won't get his hands on this." The other one crouched next to her and slipped the gun from the small of her back. "This thing'll go for a pretty penny. And what will Emil have to show for his adventure? Maybe a broken neck. So shut up about it and get your head in the game."

"Me? You're getting hot over a gun. Check her pulse and let's go," Grumpy pouted.

"I'm supposed to check her for weapons. Thoroughly." The man leaned across Cara. A large hand cupped her behind. It slid up over her waistband, and then turned decisively, groping its way down her crack. Nausea sloshed into her throat. Rage renewed her strength.

She gritted against a scream and flipped fast. Her thumb found a shaved man's light blue eye and sank to the first knuckle.

His arms shot wide. The gun clattered to the ground. A high-pitched shriek split the pristine morning.

The ends of her finger became claws, digging and holding tight.

The man wrapped both his hands around her wrist. A biting grip sank into one of her ankles and tugged. She couldn't pop the man's eyeball from the socket and maintain the seal on her wound.

As soon as her finger departed the crying man's eyeball, he released her wrist and cupped his eye.

The grump at her ankle vented a string of Swedish curses she knew too well. His upper lip crinkled into a vicious sneer. The wide sole of his boot lifted into the air, its strike aimed at her knee.

Cara's breath stalled as though she'd lost the grip on the hole in her chest.

A faraway shot displaced the air with a crack.

It yanked both her and her knee demolisher's attention to the right. The windshield of the car careening down the driveway shattered. Red sprayed the rear windshield. The car pulled sharply to the left, dipped into a ditch, and slammed to a stop. A whine from the vehicle's horn announced the loss of Emil.

The man gripping her ankle released it and hit the ground.

His bullet found the center of his forehead anyway. Cara averted her gaze from the decimation. The third bullet sliced through the air silencing the man whose eye she'd jabbed out of the socket.

Her gaze screened the sky for the Base Branch HELO but saw none. If it hadn't been them, it must have been Luck. And if it hadn't been Base Branch, they needed to get here fast.

"Din djävla hora!" Markus bellowed from inside the barn. "I kill your lover."

A toxic mix of adrenaline and fear forced Cara to her knees. The world swiveled at odd angles. Lying down had been so much easier. She blinked at the dizziness. Still, her silver pistol jogged in her vision, and her finger found it after a few attempts. It snuggled into the cradle of her hand, bolstering her flagging strength.

Good thing. Shoving to her feet used every bit of it.

Cara walked on rubber legs away from the dark barn door. She tried to ease each step onto the grass quietly around the far side of the barn. The back corner the other end where the saddles and pitchforks littered the interior wall seemed miles away.

"Where are you, Hora?" Markus screamed. "Your lover is dying."

One step at a time, Cara pressed forward.

When the first in the series of hollows in the old wood appeared, Cara nearly wept with relief. The last two steps were like the final release at the crest of a roller coaster. She nestled her eye to the hollow and peered inside.

In the far corner, two bodies lay on horse blankets. Forgotten IV lines protruded from their arms. One had a crooked line of thick stitches across his neck. The other's belly hung loose, stitches never given. Bloody rags covered their faces.

In the center of the room, Tyler's battered body thrashed against the bonds, carving deeper into the gouges on his wrists. He bit at the rope coiled around his mouth and worked it down with his teeth and sweaty bicep.

Marina wasn't among the bodies, nor was she hanging near Tyler. She wasn't anywhere, not that Cara could see. Neither was Tor.

Markus hid behind a large wooden column at the aisle. He aimed a pistol at the open barn door.

The corners of Cara's mouth twitched.

She centered the barrel of her gun in a lower hollow and fired five shots.

Each one struck one of Markus's vital organs. He hit the manure as if the shots liquefied his insides. Since two of the bullets lodged in the man's skull, she didn't wait.

Cara tucked the gun into the front of her pants, used the wall for leverage, and then staggered toward Tyler. She plunged through the barn door but hugged the first open stall to keep from collapsing.

"Cara!" Tyler's cry was hoarse. Weak or not, it strummed her heart. Tears she hadn't allowed tumbled down her face.

His gaze, hidden behind swollen and split brows, roamed her head to toe. That sturdy jaw she'd come to rely upon quaked once and then steadied.

"About time." He smiled.

"Me?" Cara laughed and sobbed. "I expected a higher body count from a Base Branch operative."

He shrugged. A grimace followed. "Bastards waited to pounce until I was jerking it in the shower."

"So really it's all my fault?" Cara looked for something to get him down. There was no way she could lift him in her condition. Her limbs quivered from holding herself upright.

Tyler gave a shallow laugh. "What do you say I let you make it up to me?"

"Sounds good."

A wooden sawhorse acted as a saddle holder for two large horned saddles. Cara shuffled over and shoved them onto the ground. She pulled the trestle along, praying her lungs would withstand the work. The finger inside her body and the others around it had fallen asleep a while ago. Every inhale returned less and less oxygen.

"Cara, stop. Sit down."

If she'd had the breath, she'd have told him the dominant stuff only worked in the bedroom, and only to a certain degree. Instead, each trudged step gave her answer.

"Stubborn woman. Passing out won't help either of us."

A chill thrashed its way through Cara's torso, split, and veered down her extremities, but she pushed on. Getting Tyler down and his leg elevated was as critical as her getting to a hospital right the fuck now. With each breath, energy seeped from her body. Her fingertips tingled. The edges of the barn blurred.

She dragged one foot at a time through the hay and muck, creating deep trenches in her wake. Then she towed the heavy wooden A-frame, its four feet creating far more drag. The closer she got to him, the slower her progress became. Through every step, her gaze never left Tyler.

His ocean deep eyes never wavered. They pulled her forward. He lent her strength and courage through the terror. Because each breath grew more and more shallow.

Finally, she stood—hunched—inches from his blood-streaked body. His scent tempted her with faint whiffs, more like a hazy, beautiful dream than reality. With one hand on the sawhorse and one plugging the hole in her chest, and doing a shitty job of it, she could touch him. If she let go of either, she wouldn't have the energy to grab them again.

Cara leaned forward. A bone-deep throb started in her chest and traveled throughout her skeleton, but she didn't pull back. She needed to touch him, to make certain he was real and alive. Her forehead grazed the top of his thigh. Heat radiated from his skin nearly burning to the touch. Cara pressed her face against him, soaking up the warmth. She was so cold.

Tears slipped silently down her cheeks. "I'm sorry."

"It's all your fault," Tyler whispered.

Her gaze shifted from the ground up his magnificent, battered body and met his gaze. She'd apologize again if she could. The weight on her chest wouldn't allow it.

"It's your fault I fell in love with you, Cara."

She smiled. She sure tried anyway.

Cara's knees buckled. Her fingers slipped off the wood and landed in swill.

"Cara Lee, that wasn't the reaction I was going for. Look at me," Tyler screamed.

Before she could give her body instructions, it made its own by flopping her onto her back at his feet. At least she could look at him until the tunnel of her vision closed completely.

"You will live, damnit."

She hoped she did for Rin, for Luck, for Tyler, and for herself.

I love you, she mouthed before the world went black.

Chapter Nineteen

"No!" Tyler's voice slammed into the barn walls and ricocheted with disturbing force. He tore at the binding and welcomed the rip of his flesh in turn. His broken skin, ribs, teeth, and leg were nagging bug bites in comparison to the torture of watching the woman he loved slowly die and knowing he was helpless to stop it.

This was what Markus had been after for so many hours. His agony. His relent. He'd give the man anything for which he asked if he'd save Cara. But the bastard's brain littered the ground only feet from where Cara now lay struggling with short, gurgling breaths.

Just because he hadn't been able to free his wrists from the bindings in the last twelve hours didn't mean he'd give up.

Tyler contracted his biceps, pulled himself up to the rope, and gnashed at it with his teeth. The loose things pried impotently at the tightly woven threads. Muscles in his arms quaked so hard it jarred fresh blood from his mouth. Pulpy hemp mixed with copper and churned his empty stomach, but he kept at it.

The roar of an engine and the kick of gravel filled him with hope. For the duration of his torture, there had been six men. He'd accounted for them with the gunshots. That and Cara had arrived in a vehicle, which someone besides her had driven. He'd guessed Luck but hadn't figured out why the hell the guy had abandoned her, fleeing with the car as soon as the shit hit the fan.

He let his arms give way, gritted against the stabbing pains all over his body, inhaled, and did something he'd never done before.

"Help! We need help! In here!"

Dread filled him on the second round of pleas. He didn't worry the enemy was coming to get them. He realized that no matter how fast they drove, it wouldn't be fast enough to save Cara.

His mouth stretched in an inhuman bellow of rage and dread.

"Tyler?" Luck rounded the open barn door and skidded to a stop. "Cara? No, shit. No."

"Help her," Tyler begged. Even though he knew they couldn't save her, he refused to give up.

Logistics were his thing. Cara needed an IV. She needed the hole in her chest plugged. They could have found those things for the job in the house if those bastards hadn't wrecked his entire first-aid stash. After that, they could drive like the devil chased their asses with flaming torches.

Rin barreled through the door. Luck turned and caught her around the waist. He tried to block the girl's view.

There wasn't time for grief.

"Luck, move," Tyler barked. "Rin, you both keep your shit together. She's not dead yet. It's our job to keep her that way."

Once kicked out of his stupor, Luck sprinted the distance with Rin a breath behind him. He propped Cara on her side, bullet wound down, and positioned Rin to hold her mother there. The guy flung the sawhorse near Tyler's feet like it weighed less than a pound. When Cara dragged it from across the barn, it seemed to weigh a thousand.

"This is going to hurt like a motherfucker." Luck climbed onto the frame and stood eye level with him.

"Do it," Tyler ordered.

The man yanked a serrated knife from the sheath at his thigh, stretched tall, and sliced at the rope. The sharp blade and gravity did the rest. Luck banded his arms around Tyler's torso. A bomb detonated inside his chest, but Tyler bit his lips to muffle the cry. Luck stepped down from the sawhorse. Stars twinkled and multiplied, filling Tyler's vision.

"Tyler." The delicate whisper pulled him back from the brink of unconsciousness. He leaned on the sturdy guy, his good leg, sought the source of the whisper, and prayed it wasn't his mind playing tricks on him.

When he found Cara lying on the dirty ground, her eyes were closed, and her beautiful face was as white as her daughter's shirt, where her mother's blood hadn't stained it.

As broken inside and out as he was, something inside Tyler fit into place in that moment of pure desperation. A sense of peace washed over him. She fought for him. He'd fight for her to the very end.

"Rin, move her shirt from over the wound. We need something plastic to place over it. Luck, look in that kit in the corner by the bodies."

"You'll fall," Luck argued.

Tyler shoved the man away, surprised his body backed him up. He hit the ground like a fifty-pound sack of feed, but it kicked the other guy into action. Using elbows and one knee, Tyler crawled to Cara.

He stroked her pale face with his bound hands. Streaks of his blood colored her cheeks. Her skin cooled his fingertips. "Cara, you will live. Do you hear me? You will live."

Tears welled in Rin's eyes, but she bit them back with a look of sheer determination and a solid bite on her lower lip.

"Here." Luck landed on his knees next to Rin with an unopened pack of surgical gloves.

"Lay the palm of one over the wound and hold it there." The package shrieked open inches from Tyler's ear. He didn't watch Luck. Instead, he listened to Cara's breathing and watched her face.

Luck adjusted the glove several times before suction caught with a sure pop of the thin plastic. Within seconds, the color in Cara's lips brightened. Her breaths still came in far too shallow draws for his liking.

"We need an..." The familiar *whop, whop* of helicopter blades drove Tyler's battered heart into his throat. "We need that bird. Luck, go wave it down. Burn the house to the ground if you have to. Just get their attention. There's room for them to land in the field."

Before he could say more, Luck's boot treads retreated.

Rin's eyes widened to the size of saucers.

"We can do this." Tyler wrapped his arms around Cara. "I'll hold her. You go to the corner and look for an unused IV. If it's not there, you'll have to go to the house."

Her gaze sliced in the direction of the bodies and then jumped back. Her cheeks drooped. "They're dead." She hadn't looked at Markus's body behind her, not once, since she'd followed Luck past it.

"Thank fuck. If I could, I'd kill them again.
Now go. You can do it. You're as strong as your
mother is."

The tears clouding Rin's eyes fell in earnest.
Her head shook back and forth, but she also stood,
balled her fists, and marched around the corpses.

Tyler tightened his arms around Cara, held
the glove in place, and pressed his lips to her cold
mouth. He levered back and watched for any
reaction, but this was no fairy tale.

"I don't see any here. They're all used," Rin
hollered from the other side of the barn.

"Look in the house. Through the back door,
in the kitchen, in the large pantry."

Rin sprinted past the bodies and headed for
the door, while Tyler willed Cara to live.

"You're the strongest person I've ever met.
Don't pansy out on me now. Cara, do you want to
live? Show me you want to live?" He shook her.
Despair crept into his words. "Do you want to live?"

Cara's throat bobbed once and then again.

"Promise to make it worth my trouble?" The
words were reedy and took several breaths for her
to complete, but they were the best words he'd ever
heard.

"I promise to love you every day of the rest of
my life."

"Yes," she breathed.

She breathed, which was all he needed her to
do right now.

The beat of the HELO's blades grew nearer.
He honestly didn't care if Luck had resorted to
burning the Sanford's house to get their attention.
Knowing the stakes, the couple might have made
the same decision. Maybe.

He held her as firmly and gently as he could
and pressed his forehead to hers. Several seconds

later, her head turned as though she were looking for something. "Tucker..."

He couldn't make out her last word. "What about Tucker?"

"HELO." One side of her mouth quirked into a lazy smirk.

"Thank you." A wave of relief washed over Tyler. He thanked God. He thanked Cara. He thanked everyone who would help him save this woman.

"Found one. I think I have everything." Rin knelt next to her mother and gasped. "You're awake."

"Rin." Cara's face didn't show the smile in her voice.

Everything she did was sluggish and reaffirmed in him the haste gone at the moment following her consciousness.

"I don't know how to put in an IV." Rin looked up and down her mother's arm.

"Swab the top of her hand."

The girl bit her top lip, this time, narrowed her gaze, and sought the small iodine packet in the IV pack. He talked Rin through the steps of inserting the tube, securing it for transport, and elevating the bag.

"Hell of a job," Tyler offered.

"That was all you." Rin blew the flyaways from her forehead.

"Teamwork," Cara offered.

"Quiet, you." Tyler pinned her with his gaze. "Conserve your oxygen."

Cara held up a finger.

"What is it?"

Sunlight streamed into the barn. Instinctively, Tyler covered Cara with his body. Luck ran through the large double doors with stretchers stacked one atop the other, carried on the other end by Kite, a Base Branch agent he knew by reputation only. The guy was a master of stealth incursion. And wanted dead by several enemy groups for the massive damage he'd inflicted with no warning.

Khani Slaughter rounded the corner with her gun aimed. She swept the area, assessing the threat level for herself. King Street, the man taking her back across the pond where she'd come from, covered her six.

"You couldn't wait until I was out of the country to bleed, Tyler?" Khani scoffed.

"Sorry to disappoint, ma'am" —Tyler uncovered Cara— "but she needs your attention way more than I do."

"Lung shot," Khani hissed in her haughty British accent as she addressed the wound. "Nice stabilization for her. What about you?" She worked while she talked, pulling the tape from a bag and securing the edges of the glove to Cara's chest.

"Plop me on the stretcher and let's go." Tyler watched the able-bodied men set down the small pallets and judge the situation.

"First, we need to cover your nuts," King chimed in with his own British—but much less proper—accent. He pulled the green shirt from his torso, revealing his vest, and tossed the cotton at Tyler. It landed on his hip and caused a jolt of pain he hadn't felt since grabbing hold of Cara.

Khani crouched low and leaned over Cara. "I'm going to need you two to let go so we can leave."

Neither of their hands loosened, and actually, Cara's tightened. She pulled his ear to her mouth. "Where are Tor and," she stalled, "and Marina?"

"Who?" he whispered back.

"Markus's brother and the other girl they were torturing?"

"None of the men here was his brother, and there was no one else."

"Luck," Cara called.

He rushed to her side looking more like an excited and simultaneously terrified boy than the tough blond-headed man he was.

"Check the premises for Tor and Marina. Watch the video on my phone and you'll know what I'm talking about."

Luck nodded at Cara's orders.

"If you're leaving with us," Khani announced before he left the barn, "we're wheels up in three."

"You can let me go now." When he didn't release her, she added, "So we can leave." Cara's breath danced across his cheek.

He had a thousand questions. Who were those people and how did they calculate into her life? More importantly, did she feel at all about him how he felt about her? But now wasn't the time.

"Just don't leave me," Tyler demanded.

"I won't," she promised.

The moment they rolled her onto her back, Cara lost consciousness.

Chapter Twenty

Someone grabbed Cara's upper arm and squeezed hard. She jerked from the hold and reached for her CZ. The IV stabbing into her hand stopped her cold, along with the realization she was in a hospital bed and an automatic blood pressure cuff was the culprit strangling her arm. Deeply rooted pain pulsed through her chest and diffused through each arm. Wires sprouted out of her oh-so-sexy gown held together by one snap on her right side. A grimace contorted Cara's face.

Then her gaze landed on the mussed brown hair and bruised forehead resting only inches from her pressure cuff. His hand lay outstretched next to his head. Thick gauze encircled his wrist.

He wore his own hospital issued ensemble, complete with legwear. A black hip-to-calf brace wrapped around his gauze-packaged leg, which he'd propped on a padless chair opposite the one on which he sat—slumped. Gooey warmth washed her pain to the recesses. Her fingers stretched out to touch him, as desperate for the contact as she'd been in the barn.

Her fingers hovered over his hair. Every place she looked, rich blue and black marks stained his skin.

A low vibration fluttered the sheets between them. The screen of her phone lit. Cara read the incoming text.

Tucker: Our boys are moving in. How's Cara?

The information didn't make sense. She had no idea how long she'd been unconscious and what had transpired during that time. Had they found Marina? Cara lifted the phone and accessed her text log.

Something shifted in the far corner of the room, stealing her fuzzy focus. Luck reclined on a loveseat. His legs sprawled off the front because Rin snuggled to his side on the other cushion. Her daughter burrowed her sweet face under the cleft of Luck's chin and sighed.

Cara smiled and returned to the phone and a conversation between Tyler and Base Branch director Vail Tucker. The feed started at 6:00 p.m. the previous day, and it was 4:20 p.m.—whatever day it was.

Tucker: Located the signal where Marina's video is being transmitted in Sweden. It's in the middle of Brödraskapet territory. Oliver and Hunter are en route.

Tyler: There's a story here. Luck won't talk. Says it's Cara's to tell.

Tucker: Any change in her condition?

Tyler: No.

Tucker: She's a fighter.

Tyler: Hell yeah, she is.

Tucker: They landed.

Tyler: Luck says to hold them off.

Tucker: What if this girl is going through what you did?

Tyler: Tell them to watch their asses, even though they won't listen.

Tucker: You were the sensible one in that outfit.

Tyler: Keep me updated.

Cara's gaze caressed Tyler for several minutes. She enjoyed the rise and fall of his chest and the bump of his pulse against his neck...even if it was marred with bruises. What if Marina was going through what he did? What if she wasn't?

No matter how much she denied it, the girl had burned her before.

She needed more information. Tucker did too. Cara typed.

Cara: It's Cara. Hold your boys off, it's a trap.

Tucker: Glad you're back. I need details.

Cara: You may reconsider hiring me once you hear them, but I'm ready to tell.

Tucker: Be up there within the hour.

She looked at Tyler and typed once more.

Cara: If you still want to hire me after you hear the story, then I have a non-negotiable condition.

Tucker: Name it.

Cara: I plan to be with Tyler. There can't be a clause that keeps us from being together.

Tucker: If you haven't noticed, you're not the only couple we employ. We can accommodate you.

She set the phone on the bed and reached for the man she loved. Her fingertips grazed the unruly tips of his hair. The delicate contact trumpeted a rush of warmth and tingles up her arm. A drunken sense of peace settled over her chest. She delved deeper. Lush, knotted strands caressed her hand. Heat from his scalp radiated into her palm. Tears stung, threatening release.

Tyler yawned and then groaned. His finger stretched forward in a blind search, and when he didn't find what he sought, he straightened with the grace of a ninety-year-old man. Her hand slid from his hair to the prickles of a sprouting beard. His closed lips buffered his grunts and grumbles. His sleepy, swollen gaze swung her way. Through the puffy, butterfly-band-aided skin, he gave her a smile that curled her toes and hugged her heart at the same time.

"You should be in a bed of your own." Cara's voice shook with unadulterated love for this man.

His large hand skated up the back of hers and held it firmly to his cheek.

For the first time since she'd received the horrid video, her lungs expanded with a full breath.

"We haven't been able to keep him in it." Rin grinned from her perch on the couch. "Maybe you can help?"

Cara knew he should go, prop his leg up on a bed on pillows, and take care of himself. She couldn't make the orders form on her lips, nor could she let go of his handsome face.

"I think she'll be the opposite of help. Can't blame either one of them." Luck stood and reached for Rin. When she grabbed his hand, he pulled her up and kissed the back of it. "I'm starved. Let's go get some food."

Luck tossed a wink at Cara, pulling a blush to her cheeks.

"Thank you." Rin bounded over to the open side of her bed and kissed her forehead.

"For?" Cara caught her daughter's hand, pulled her back, and placed a kiss on her cheek.

"Being okay." Rin smiled.

"My pleasure." Cara watched her kids exit the room and pull the door closed behind them. Her gaze found Tyler's. "You really should elevate your leg higher than your heart."

"I left you once. I'm not doing it again." Tyler
pulled her hand from his face. His fingers danced
over her skin. "Push, if you want. I can handle it.
We'll take it slow. I can wait, but I won't give up on
you."

She gritted against the agony to come and
pulled her hand from Tyler's. Both palms braced on
the bed, Cara lifted her bottom off the fitted sheet
and shifted toward the far side of the bed.

Tyler's smile faltered.

Her full breaths carried her through the pain.
When she could move again, she patted the bed
next to her.

"I can't wait. I've been stubborn and scared
long enough. I'm ready for you." A smile stretched
her mouth. "Ready to snuggle, at least."

He eyed her head to toe with a teasing grin.
"I'm supposed to get up there, right next to your
sweet, hot skin, and only snuggle?"

"You're a highly capable man."

"I hope this feat doesn't prove you wrong."
Tyler half winked—because his eye already hung at
half-mast—and hoisted himself onto the bed from
the chair. He paused several times in transition,
breathing in slowly through his nose and out his
mouth.

Finally, his body snuggled alongside hers. He
draped a bandaged arm over her shoulder and
slowly eased her against him. A hiss spit from
between his teeth.

"We don't have to do this now."

"I haven't felt this good in two days."

"Sounds it," she scoffed.

"You're not moving, Cara. I've lived through a
ton of crazy shit, and I've never been as terrified as
I was when you…" His words caught, and he shook

his head. He cleared his throat. "A little pain in the ribs, I can handle."

"Are they broken?"

"Nah." He waved her off. "Only four. Markus slapped like a bitch."

"Right." Cara shook her head.

The door opened, and a nurse stepped into the room.

Tyler's hand shot up, stalling the man. "Her BP is seventy over a hundred and eight, temp is ninety-eight point two, heart rate is seventy-three. A little high for her, but I'm beside her, so can you blame the woman?" He gestured to their aligned bodies and waggled his puffy brow. "What can I say? I get to her."

"Your friends tried to call me off too, but you know I'm going to have to check her." The nurse smirked, crossed his arms, but didn't continue into the room. "I'll give you ten minutes."

"Twenty," Tyler argued.

"Twelve," the nurse countered.

"We'll take it." Cara nodded her thanks. The man pulled the door closed, and she turned to Tyler. "How'd you know all that?"

"I've been keeping track." His gaze hit the floor and rolled around the room.

"What is it?"

"I want to save people, not kill them," Tyler grudgingly admitted.

"That's something to be proud of." She cradled his chin in her hand and pulled his gaze easily to hers.

"I don't want you to think I'm judging you. What you, we, do, it's ugly, but vital work. We maintain the balance."

"And saving the good guys' lives is part of that balance." Cara's heart swelled. "I'm glad you're figuring it out. Glad we both are." She placed a kiss on her thumb and then rubbed it over his lips.

"I really wish we were able bodied right now," Tyler growled.

"Me too." Her words came out more breathlessly than she would have liked. In an effort to turn down the pulse growing between her thighs, Cara steered the conversation in a different direction. "So are you planning to wear a white coat?" Because that would be damn hot too."

"I'm not ready to give up my battle gear, even though I won't be in it for a while. Khani is a field medic. She's leaving soon."

"We'll need someone to replace her." Cara hiked a brow. "You'd be a natural."

"You're taking the job?" His split lips formed a grin.

"If the job takes me."

"It will." He nodded. But he hadn't yet heard her story. "Mine will take some extensive training," he continued, "but I'm up for it. What the hell else can I do for the next few months?"

"I have a few ideas." Cara laced her fingers with his.

"You're bound to get me in trouble."

She shrugged and grimaced. "My past will be swarming around the room shortly."

"Until then, lean on me." Tyler pulled her into the crook of his arm.

The worry over the skeletons to free fell silent. His heartbeat thumped assuredly in her ear. Hers calmed to match it. Being in Tyler's arms was the closest thing to coming home she'd ever experienced. And she never wanted the feeling to go away.

"How about I lean here forever? And when you need to, you can lean back?"

Tyler released a shuttering breath.

"That's good for me, darlin'."

"I love you, Tyler."

"I was wondering but wasn't going to rush you."

"I love you," she said again.

"Hot damn. I love you too." He kissed the top of her head and cradled her face in his big hand...

Where she'd stay forever.

VARIATIONS
A BASE BRANCH NOVEL

Decisions split paths. Bad decisions compound and suddenly you are no more than variations of yourself.

Marina Sorensen rots in a prison of her own making. The bars are the thick arms and meaty hands of Brödraskapet thugs who make money selling her body. Her guilt is the unbreakable shackle. Loneliness is her ever tightening noose. Trading her life for the survival of another is her only salvation.

For Base Branch operative Oliver Knight an eliminate and rescue mission in hostile territory against a brotherhood of brutal sons-of-bitches is another adventure. Downtime between missions in foreign locales with exotic women is worth dodging a few bullets. There is also the sense of duty and pride in a job well done.

He and his buddy rescue Marina and are blindsided by the striking, broken woman who mistakes them for Stronghold Tech. Before they can figure out how she knows about the elite securities team or find and eliminate their mark, the enemy discovers their hideout. Capture would be a fate worse than death and it looms so close Oliver and Marina can french it.

Betrayals meet harsh light and the fun-loving soldier is forced to face cruel reality. His damsel in distress is the one to blame, especially when Stronghold forces show, adding chaos to the kabooms. The dire situation turns deadly and Marina holds the key.

If only Oliver can stop loving and hating her long enough to get the answers.

FOR ALL TO SEE
A BUREAU NOVEL

Pristine waters and purified evil.

Two by two, dark-haired beauties vanish only to reappear as hanging, plundered corpses. The Virgin Islands boast diamond-white beaches, lush green mountains, a rich cultural heritage—and a brutal killer.

Three years on the "Field-Dresser" case and Special Agent Nathan Brewer is days away from catching the bastard—if he can convince a certain brunette to trust him. Only the woman is more likely to take a casual stroll on the surface of the sun.

After fleeing her troubles in the United States for the quiet life of a school teacher on the island of Tortola, Madelyn Garrett never imagined she'd be fixated upon by pure evil.

In a fight for her life—with a dwindling number of friends—she must rely on her cunning and Nathan's skills for survival.

Megan Mitcham was born and raised among the live oaks and shrimp boats of the Mississippi Gulf Coast, where her enormous family still calls home. She attended college at the University of Southern Mississippi where she received a bachelor's degree in curriculum, instruction, and special education. For several years Megan worked as a teacher in Mississippi. She married and moved to South Carolina and began working for an international non-profit organization as an instructor and co-director.

In 2009 Megan fell in love with books. Until then, books had been a source for research or the topic of tests. But one day she read *Mercy* by Julie Garwood. And oh, Mercy, she was hooked!

Megan lives in Southern Arkansas where she pens heart pounding romantic thriller novels and window-steaming erotic romance. For information on releases and giveaways subscribe at meganmitcham.com!

Facebook: AuthorMeganMitcham
Twitter: @MeganMMMitcham
Pinterest: MeganMitcham5
Goodreads: Megan_Mitcham
Website: www.meganmitcham.com